'You're carrying my child, so you can forget any ideas you've got about cutting me out of its life.'

Reb continued, 'You might not have much of an opinion of me, but you're way off base if you think I'm going to walk away from my own flesh and blood.'

Amanda-Jayne forced herself to speak calmly and civilly. 'Am I to understand that you're determined to contribute to the baby's upbringing?'

Reb mentioned a monthly sum he considered reasonable and she nearly staggered with surprise. 'I'm afraid there's a condition to my offer...'

Amanda-Jayne swallowed hard. 'What?'

'You have to marry me to get it.'

EXPECTING!

**She's sexy,
successful…
and
PREGNANT!**

Relax and enjoy our series of stories about spirited women and gorgeous men, whose passion results in pregnancies…sometimes unexpected! Of course, the birth of a baby is always a joyful event, and we can guarantee that our characters will become besotted mums and dads—but what happened in those nine months before?

Share the surprises, emotions, dramas and suspense as our parents-to-be come to terms with the prospect of bringing a new little life into the world…

All will discover that the business of making babies brings with it the most special love of all…

EXPECTING! continues next month with *The Baby Verdict* by Cathy Williams.

THE BABY DEAL

BY
ALISON KELLY

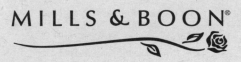

MILLS & BOON®

My thanks to
Bernice for her assistance with the research,
and to Bob, for knowing about '82 Fords

*First published in Great Britain 1999
Harlequin Mills & Boon Limited,
Eton House, 18-24 Paradise Road, Richmond, Surrey TW9 1SR*

© Alison Kelly 1999

ISBN 0 263 81781 4

*Set in Times Roman 10½ on 11 pt.
01-9909-57717 C1*

*Printed and bound in Spain
by Litografía Rosés, S.A., Barcelona*

PROLOGUE

TEARS of shame rolled down Amanda-Jayne's face at the realisation that after years spent endeavouring to be the perfect daughter and then the perfect wife she'd spent the last few hours behaving like a perfect tramp.

She wanted to die on the spot.

No, she didn't!

She could just imagine how the newspapers would report the circumstances of her death: DIVORCED SOCIALITE FOUND DEAD AFTER A NIGHT OF PASSION WITH HOME-TOWN BAD BOY.

The humiliating implications of that thought had her quickly but silently swinging her feet to the floor as her eyes struggled to adjust to the pitch-blackness of her surroundings. Her tears weren't helping the situation, but unfortunately her instinctive recognition of lush, quality carpet beneath her as she lowered herself onto her hands and knees was as much another source of despair as it was a relief. The possibility that this was a hotel where she'd previously stayed and might be recognised by staff—or, worse, one of the guests—was almost as disturbing as her original fear that, in keeping with her appalling behaviour, once she orientated herself she'd find herself in some two-bit flea trap.

Seconds later, though, her night vision sharpened enough to reveal that while the hotel was obviously a five-star one it wasn't, thank goodness, one she patronised. Now all she had to do was try and find her clothes and escape before the naked man adorning the mattress she'd just vacated woke up.

Trying to keep one eye on his prone form as she crawled

on hands and knees, following the trail of her clothes, wasn't easy. Especially not when her outraged conscience was screaming loud enough to wake the dead. Oh, dear Lord, who'd have thought giving in to her married friends' demands that she celebrate her divorce with a 'girls night out' would end up like this? Certainly not anyone who knew her. At least she fervently hoped not.

Spying her bra peeking out from beneath a pair of floor-strewn black boxers, Amanda-Jayne felt her face flame in the darkness. Snatching it up, she hastily slipped it on but, rather than reassuring her, the recovery of the garment somehow made what she was doing seem even more tawdry than what she'd already done. On the verge of screaming that it was shame, not excitement generated from the memory of how she and the garment had become separated, that was causing the disturbing heat within her, she caught herself. Oh, Lord, she couldn't afford for what modicum of sanity she still possessed to abandon her now. She had to get out of here before he woke up; now wasn't the time for tears or self-recrimination.

Several moments of head-swivelling perusal of the nearby area revealed no sign of her panties. Where the devil were her pa—? Her belly clenched even before her eyes strayed to the tangle of sheets. Oh, no! Uh-uh. There was *no way* that she was going to climb back in there looking for them.

What on earth had possessed her? How could she have acted so out of character; done something so…so rash? Rash? *Rash?* Ha! Who was she trying to kid? *Cheap* was the only word to describe her actions. She must have been drunk, despite the fact she'd only had a couple of drinks… Perhaps the stress of the last year had caused some sort of abnormal biophysical reaction. That *could* happen… couldn't it? Of course it could! It must have. After all, she wasn't a big drinker, so surely if she'd drunk so much that tonight had been solely the result of alcohol consumption then by rights she should be in the last stages of alcoholic poisoning or clinically dead by now.

It wasn't just what she'd done, but with whom she'd done it. This was a thousand times worse than waking up and finding she'd gone to bed with a well-respected businessman or even a famous celebrity or noted lawyer. Apparently she'd been so drunk she'd gone to bed with…with— No! It didn't bear thinking about. Although she supposed she should take some comfort from the fact that by committing this act of lunacy outside the perimeters of her usual social circle she'd spared herself the risk of ever having to face him again. Unless, of course, she took *complete* leave of her senses, bought a Harley and started running with a group of bikers!

If only she'd declined to go 'celebrating' with her friends. If only she hadn't refused to go home when Rachel and Penelope had left. 'If only I could find my stupid dress,' she muttered, flinging aside the male shirt she'd mistaken for her clothing.

A throaty male growl suddenly rumbled through the darkness, momentarily stopping her heart.

Then the bed base emitted several soft whimpers, suggesting movement from its occupant. Holding her breath, Amanda-Jayne remained on her hands and knees, face buried in the carpet, praying devoutly that her naked derrière wasn't visible from the bed. Not that it hadn't already been closely scrutinised, stroked and admired by the man in question, she mused miserably, not daring to move. If he thought she'd already left he'd probably roll over and go back to sleep. Of course it was possible he *was* still asleep, in which case she was wasting valuable time remaining here face down, butt up doing nothing!

Still not game to risk breathing, she furtively raised her head enough to peek over the foot of the bed at the sheet-draped nude male, only to quickly shut her eyes in a bid to discourage reminders of how intimately acquainted she and the still dozing Adonis had recently become. She clamped a hand over her mouth to keep back what she would have liked to believe was a moan of despair, but the sad truth was it was more likely generated by lust—and lack of oxygen. Much as she might be feeling ashamed enough to die, there was no denying the man who'd managed to get her to abandon the morals of a lifetime had a body to die for. *Not that that was any excuse for her wanton behaviour.*

But what she really wanted to know was how a motorbike-riding rebel from her home town had gained entry into the fashionably chic, members-only Sydney nightclub anyway. Even *she'd* been on a waiting list for two years before her membership had been sanctioned. Well, she'd certainly be having something to say to the management about the lax security—

Oh, God! What was she thinking?

She wasn't going to mention this incident, or what led up to it, to anyone! *Ever.* In fact…she lit the face of her watch…as of 4:51 a.m. October the twentieth, October the nineteenth had not existed this year!

CHAPTER ONE

LETHAL'S barking drew Reb's attention to the car pulling alongside the petrol bowsers. Positioned flat on his back below the underbelly of old Mrs Kelly's classic FJ Holden, his view was somewhat restricted, but he could see enough of the new arrival's sporty wheels and hubcaps to know the driver wasn't a regular customer.

Good. At 5:40 p.m. on New Year's Eve the last thing he needed was another hard-luck story and a plea for a mechanical miracle. He should've closed up forty minutes ago, but he'd been a soft touch for Mrs K's desperate appeal that he fix her exhaust so she could drive to the cemetery to picnic with her two-decades-dead husband for their anniversary tomorrow. Still, while he might have a soft spot for zany elderly locals, he didn't feel any obligation to humour impatient tourists who kept their hand clamped on the horn, inciting Lethal to vocal mania.

'Shut up, Leth!' he bellowed, turning his head to view the bottom of the staircase leading to the upper-level apartment and willing his cousin to respond to the ongoing racket from dog and horn.

After several seconds of the continued ear-splitting duet and no sign of the presumably still sulking Savannah, Reb let out a frustrated curse. At this rate he'd be lucky to get out of here in time to have one beer by midnight, much less make it to Gunna's party. Shoving the trolley out from under the car, he jackknifed to his feet.

'Can it, Lethal! You brainless mutt!' The barking stopped, but the dog continued to jump around on its hind legs like a demented giant rabbit then plunked his paws on Reb's shoulders to eyeball him with a play-with-me grin.

9

'Lord save me from slobbering canines and moody, petulant females,' he grumbled, before saying, '*Down*, Lethal.'

The firmness of the command brought an immediate response, and one finger pointed in the direction of the canine trampoline sent the dog scampering there. Of course the cessation of the dog's antics made the ongoing blaring of the horn that much more obvious and grating to Reb's day-worn temper.

'Yeah, right-oh, mate!' he bellowed, wiping the grease from his hands down his overalls as he strode from the workshop. 'Keep your shirt on! Just 'cos you drive a sports car doesn't make you—' His outburst was stalled by the same shocked disbelief that brought his legs to a standstill.

To say he was stunned would have been the greatest understatement since Creation. In fact the only other person he'd have been more surprised to find sitting behind the wheel of the sleek midnight-blue imported convertible gracing the driveway of the Browne Bike and Auto Emporium was Elvis. Presumably, though, Elvis was dead, which explained his absence, but not the beautiful, spoilt and extremely wealthy Ms Amanda-Jayne Vaughan's presence.

In the minuscule fraction of time between her swinging her Titian-haired head in his direction and the almost electrifying effect of her gaze touching him, the horn was suddenly defeated by a silence so loud Reb could have sworn his body vibrated from it. He told himself the sudden increase in his body temperature was the result of leaving the semi-coolness of the workshop and the fact he was wearing heavy cotton drill overalls in the peak of the Australian summer. His brain, however, immediately dismissed that explanation as the load of bunk it was, because as usual Amanda-Jayne Vaughan looked like every man's fantasy and Reb was unfortunately male.

Her hair was loose, restrained from her face only by the undoubtedly designer-brand sunglasses pushed onto her head, and the copper-red tresses complemented her exquisite classical beauty as Reb could imagine no other colour doing. A faint flush tinted her fair, creamy skin, but whether it was caused by irritation, the heat or self-consciousness Reb couldn't guess—although the notion that it might be the latter was downright ridiculous. *As if the Vaughans had ever been averse to being the centre of attention!* More likely Amanda-Jayne was peeved because she'd had to wait for service and was embarrassed by the events and her behaviour the last time they'd met.

Unbidden, memories of that encounter drew his gaze to the subtle swell of her breasts beneath her knit vest top and sent his arousal meter soaring. There wasn't a real lot of Amanda-Jayne Vaughan compared to the women he was usually attracted to, but for all her understated physical attributes, her highfalutin' ways and her stuck-up attitude he had to admit that she had the hottest mouth and the smoothest skin he'd ever encountered. Just the notion of exploring them both again sent his taste buds and fingers into flashback mode.

Amanda-Jayne scrambled to remember what opening line she'd used when she'd been rehearsing this moment on the drive over, but it eluded her. So too did every other bit of the calm, businesslike request she'd come here to make. She swallowed, trying to pacify both her mind and a nervous stomach that wasn't helping the situation. She also tried to ignore the fact that the convertible offered her no protection from the eyes of the man towering beside it on the passenger side. It didn't work. His insultingly slow perusal of her body ignited inner sparks which had her squirming in her seat. It was only after endless seconds of his scrutiny, when she managed to pull her own gaze from him, that she noticed her sarong skirt had fallen open and was exposing the full length of her left leg.

'Oh, my God!' She jerked the ends of the fabric together.

'Hey,' he said. 'Don't sweat it. Truth is, A.J., I could stand here all day looking at you.' His smirk was pure lust.

'Well, I can assure you I *didn't* come here to be leered at by you!'

'I can't leer, huh? Damn,' he murmured, his expression rueful as he brought it back to her face. 'Guess that probably eliminates us having hot, torrid sex from your agenda too, huh?'

It was all Reb could do not to laugh as thick-lashed brown eyes widened in a now almost beetroot face, her sexy mouth opening and closing without emitting a word. In one respect it was a disappointment because the husky timbre of her cultured voice and precise diction fascinated him—especially since he'd discovered that years of elocution hadn't limited her conversation to giving orders and civilised put-downs. Ah, no, the publicly polite Ms Vaughan's vocabulary could get real earthy in the heat of passion. However, since he was about as likely to get a second exposure to that passion as he was to be nominated as the next Prime Minister, Reb would take his fun when and where he could get it. Right now that was in the driveway of his garage and it was obvious from his unexpected customer's two-handed grip on the steering wheel and rigid posture that she wasn't comfortable, or happy about being there.

Well, all joking aside, nor was Reb.

It irked him all ends up that the stuck-up little snob, who'd first caught his attention back in the days when she'd spent vacations from her posh boarding-school toting spoilt rich boys around town and driving poor local guys like him out of their lusting minds, could still get him all hot and bothered. Oh, sure, she was even more beautiful and sexy than she had been at fifteen, but Reb figured that, having recently received a shot of her charms, he should have been immune to her. That he wasn't didn't sit well with him.

Especially not when she was sitting in his driveway, in her expensive car, and looking as if she'd been thrust into her worst nightmare. Then again, having to pass through, let alone stop in this part of town was probably enough to send a Vaughan into months of psychiatric counselling.

'Gotta say this is a surprise, A.J.—'

'My name is *not* A.J.'

'So what's the deal? Your family just heard a bridge got put in in the twenties and curiosity had you itching to see how the other half of Vaughan's Landing lived?'

'No, I—'

'Nah,' he cut in. 'I didn't think so. Your lot can't even bring themselves to acknowledge there *is* another half. I reckon the last time any of the illustrious Vaughans crossed into this part of town must've been on horseback in the 1890s, when old Walter Vaughan founded the place.'

Her expression was a combination of impatience, condescension and definite discomfort as she flicked her gaze from the deserted road around the equally deserted petrol station. He could tell she was mentally calculating how many rungs her social status would slide if anyone happened to see her here. The urge to delay her for as long as possible in the hope that Mrs Kelly, the root of the town grapevine, would arrive to pick up the FJ while she was here was strong. But so too was the desire to get rid of her as soon as possible and once again relegate her to the deep recesses of his memory. The women at Gunna's party might lack the cool, elegant class of Amanda-Jayne Vaughan, but they would also lack her icy, superior attitude.

'So what do you want?' he asked, blocking out an egotistical voice reminding him he'd once managed to very thoroughly thaw A.J. 'Petrol or water?'

'Neither. I'm here because—'

'Never mind,' he said, now spying the worn offside rear tyre on the car. 'I can see why you're here.'

She seemed so comically astounded by his statement, Reb was more amused than insulted by her reaction. After all, in her social circle it was automatically accepted that people of his ilk uniformly had double-digit incomes and single-digit IQs and nothing he said would ever change that opinion. *Not*, he reminded himself, moving to inspect the tread wear on the front tyres, *that he gave a stuff about changing that opinion.*

Bracing the driver's-side front wheel in his hands, he gave it a solid shake. The action brought a female yelp of, 'Reb!'

The sound of his name froze him rigid, all interest in the wheel's stability instantly fleeing. His reaction was partially due to the fact that she'd finally used his name, but also because the bemused, startled tone was a blood-stopping reminder of another occasion when she'd gasped his name.

'Reb…wh-wh-what are you doing?'

He straightened, wondering if he'd imagined the faint uncertainty in her tone. The tight-lipped glare she shot him down with when he chanced a wink and said, 'Why? Shaking you up a bit, am I?' pretty much labelled his imagination as uncontrollable even before she snapped,

'Don't try and be smart!'

'Gosh darn,' he drawled facetiously, more angry with himself than her. 'There I go forgettin' my lowly station in life again. I *sure* am sorry, ma'am.'

Her chest rose on a long, exaggerated indrawn breath and Reb couldn't pull his gaze from it until it lowered on an exasperated exhale. 'If you're quite through acting the comic,' she chided, 'you might be ready to hear why I'm here.'

More like I was acting the fool! he berated himself, before saying aloud, 'Like I said, I can see why you're here.' He shook his head. 'I don't know what you're paying your regular mechanic to maintain this baby, but, sweetheart, he's ripping you off. Your two rear tyres are as bald as bowling balls and the front ones are barely legal. You're in desperate need of a wheel alignment and balance—'

'*What?*'

'I don't have the time to do that now, but swing the car into the workshop and I'll fit the new tyres.'

'But…but I don't want new—'

'Look, sweetheart, I know you wouldn't be familiar with

the saying beggars can't be choosers, but the fact is it's after closing time on New Year's Eve and there's nowhere else round here you're going to get tyres fitted before Monday.'

'Would you *please* not interrupt me and listen? *I don't need any tyres!*'

'Ha, don't kid yourself! Sweetheart, I've seen erasers with more rubber on them than this car! Now, I don't doubt you can afford the price of a defect fine, but the bottom line is those wheels are going to cause you a serious braking problem, or worse, real soon.'

He grinned. 'But lucky for you I have this thing about protecting fools from themselves, so I'm going to help you out. Now, swing your car over there and—'

'I will do no such thing,' she said hotly. 'I already know that what meets your standards of *protection* don't meet mine!'

'Oh, right, like your knowledge of tyres extends beyond knowing they're made of rubber and should be kept round,' Reb said dryly, resenting having his mechanical reputation and skills called into question.

'For your information, *Ms Vaughan*,' he continued, wondering why he simply didn't just tell her to take a hike, 'I never use anything but top-of-the-line tyres on *my* vehicles! The only reason I don't stock your brand of choice is there's no point me carrying expensive brands that none of my regulars can afford to buy. I do, however, ensure that those I stock offer excellent protection under emergency braking conditions. Something yours won't—'

'Oh, for heaven's sake! I don't care a whit about what sort of budget tyres you use! It's your choice of inferior personal protection that's a problem!'

Reb felt himself stagger. 'My *what*?'

'You heard me!'

'Yeah, but I've having a rough time keeping up with your conversational leaps.'

'Yeah? Well, if you think that's tough, try this—I'm having a baby!'

She delivered the words with a ferocity that not only stunned him, but seemed to have shocked even her for she sagged back against her seat, shaking, then buried her face in her hands.

'*You're pregnant?*' Reb wasn't so much questioning her as trying to come to terms with the idea. *Amanda-Jayne Vaughan was pregnant?* Of all the women he knew in this town Amanda-Jayne Vaughan was the last one he'd have picked to end up a single mother. It was a joke in this part of Vaughan's Landing that if a girl wasn't pregnant by the time she was eighteen her parents usually threw a party or started questioning her fertility. Sadly, the low socio-economic situation seemed to continually foster kids who repeated their parents' mistakes. But Amanda-Jayne Vaughan…

For starters she was in her late twenties and from one of the richest families in the state, which meant she should have been smart enough to avoid slip-ups and wealthy enough to cover them up if she didn't. Reb, therefore, could only assume she'd chosen to go the 'fashionable' solo mother route. He personally didn't approve of the trend, but it was nothing to him what the up-market Ms Vaughan did. Why she'd imagine he'd be the least bit interest—

Suddenly his brain began putting two and two together, arriving at an answer that brought pure panic. *Oh, hell!*

'Are…are…?' He gripped the door of her car, barely able to get the words out. 'Are you say…? *You're pregnant, to me?*'

At the minuscule nod of her head, Reb felt every drop of blood rush to his feet.

'You're having *my* baby?'

'Please keep your voice down,' she hissed. 'I have no intention—'

'You can't be!'

'That's what I said. But we're both wrong.'

This couldn't be happening to him. Nah, it was a joke! he told himself. Except the face of the woman in front of him wasn't smiling.

'Are…are you sure about this?' he heard himself ask. 'I mean, maybe you're just late. Have you seen a doctor?'

'Of course I've seen a doctor! Why else would I be here? A social visit?'

He ignored her sarcasm. 'But….but you can't mean *I'm* the father?' he protested. 'I *can't* be. I used protection. I *always* use protection. Religiously. Someone else must be the father.'

'I beg your pardon? Do you seriously believe I'd be desperate enough to nominate you as the father of my child if there was the remotest chance it could be somebody else? *Anybody* else,' she said snootily. 'And, furthermore, while I've absolutely no doubt *you* are a practising disciple of casual sex, I am not.'

That she was acting like indignation personified had Reb seeing every shade of red. 'Well, I'm sorry all ends up to offend your sensibilities, sweetheart. But I just assumed since it was so *easy* to get you in the sack that night that I wouldn't be the only guy who'd managed it.'

As much as Amanda-Jayne hated him for the comment she could well understand why he'd think as much. 'I…I was drunk that night,' she muttered, desperate to regain her dignity in her own eyes if not his.

The laugh that broke from him was scathing. 'Now there's an ironic defence for one's morals if ever I've heard one. But in *my* defence I have to say that you didn't seem all that drunk when you darted out of bed and adroitly rounded up your clothes in the dark.'

'What would you know?' she challenged. 'You were sound asleep.'

'Was I?' He smirked as the realisation dawned on her face that he'd been awake the whole time she'd been executing her soundless escape. 'If you'd asked me,' he said,

'I could've told you where your knickers and left shoe were.'

The announcement initially threw her, making her feel an even bigger fool than she obviously was, but the smug amusement on Reb Browne's face quickly prompted her to go back on the offensive. 'Really? Then why pretend to be asleep? Why didn't you say something?'

'Like what? Suggest you stay? Was that what you were hoping I'd do?'

'No!' she gasped. 'I was mortified by what I'd done! I'd never done anything like that in my life!'

'No?' He grinned. 'Then, honey, you must be a real quick study 'cos your inexperience sure didn't show.'

'You... I... How...?'

Amanda-Jayne would have liked to believe her stuttering incoherence was due entirely to outrage at the insult, but her mutilated feminine ego insisted on seizing upon the implication that, unlike her philandering ex-husband, Reb Browne *hadn't* found her lacking in bed. And he should know! For, while Anthony had taken great delight in telling her she'd not possessed a tenth of the sexual prowess of the dozen or so lovers he'd taken during their seven-year marriage, it was common knowledge that Reb Browne probably slept with more women than that in a fortnight. There—

Oh, Lord, what was she thinking? Browne's reputation wasn't a bonus, it was a serious cause for concern. Hell, it was the only reason she'd decided to advise him of the pregnancy.

When her obstetrician had asked if she knew of any genetic medical problems on the baby's father's side of the family, she'd almost passed out from dread. Not even his assurances that it was only a routine question and that even at this early stage of her pregnancy everything was progressing normally could alleviate her fears. Given that her own medical history put this pregnancy in the realms of a miracle even before one took into account the malfunctioning condom, the idea of her losing this baby was something she couldn't contemplate. No matter how embarrassing the circumstances of the conception were or how humiliating it was to have to confront this man again, she *had* to know of any and all possible conditions that might put her pregnancy at risk.

'Look,' she said, grateful for an upbringing which allowed her to summon poise, confidence and decorum even when her mind and emotions were reeling out of control. 'I'm not going to deny that I'm ashamed of my part in creating this situation. I am. Mortified, in fact. However, you have to assume some responsibility and—'

'I'm not going to marry you if that's what you're—'

A horrified shriek was the only way Reb could have described the noise that erupted from her.

'Never!' she spat. 'Not if I had to kill myself to stop it happening.'

He grinned. 'My sentiments exactly. But since I've never dodged my responsibilities in the past I'm not going to start now. So you prove I'm the father and naturally I'll pay child support.'

'I've never dodged my responsibilities in the past...' Amanda-Jayne's heart ceased beating as the words echoed in her head.

Dear Lord, was it possible her child would have a half-sibling living in Vaughan's Landing? Of course it was! Given Reb Browne's popularity with women it was entirely feasible he'd sired *more* than one other child. It was something which hadn't occurred to her. But it should have because the Brownes' history in this part of the state was almost as long as the Vaughans'. Her grandmother had once told her that in just eighty years the Browne men had probably sired more children outside marriage than the Vaughans had had hot dinners.

'Y-you've fathered other children?'

'No!'

'You *haven't?*'

'*No*. Like I told you, I *always* wear a condom. So if the reason you've turned chalk-white is because you're worrying about something besides being pregnant, you don't have to.'

'What? Oh! Oh, no. No, I wasn't worried about that.' At least she hadn't been since the doctor had given her the all-clear a week ago.

'Should *I* be?'

'What?'

'Worried about—'

'Of course not! I've only ever slept with my husband…er, ex-husband.'

'And me.' His smirk was smug, suggestive and sexy, creating a heat in Amanda-Jayne's belly which had her loins tingling even as she hovered on the verge of tears. According to the books she'd read she could expect her emotions to be at the mercy of her hormones throughout her pregnancy and possibly beyond, but there was no way on earth she was going to start crying in front of the like of Reb Browne.

'Hey, are you all right? What's wrong? Are you in pain or something?' There was genuine, almost panicked concern in the male face and voice as he crouched beside her seat. 'A.J.?'

'I'm fine.'

'Yeah, right. You look even more shell-shocked than I feel—which means you're nowhere near fine.' He studied her face for moment, muttered a string of profanities under his breath, then he pinched the bridge of his nose. 'You're fair dinkum about this, aren't you?'

He gave her no time to answer the grimly voiced question. 'Look, I mean what I said. If it's my child—'

'*It is.*'

'—I'll meet my financial responsibilities and everything else a father is supposed to…to— Aw, hell!' He looked skyward for several seconds, raking both hands through his hair, then sighed heavily and turned back to her.

'You know, I'd have an easier time grasping things if you'd come here to tell me World War Three had just started, Vaughan's Landing was at the centre of it and I had to do maintenance on the tanks. At least there's a chance I'd have been half expecting *that*,' he said dryly.

Amanda-Jayne *was* expecting World War Three—immediately once her stepmother learned she was pregnant. Not that she was ever going to admit to anyone who had sired her child. Belatedly it occurred to her that the man responsible was staring at her in the way people did when they were expecting a response. She frowned. 'What?'

'Look,' he said wearily, 'I understand we need to talk this through and obviously you're here because you're anxious to discuss the situation, but I can't. Not now. I need time to get my head around this. I asked if we could meet somewhere tomorrow night, to talk things through. Work out where we go from here.'

He sounded so sincere, so caring, it took Amanda-Jayne several seconds to comprehend what he was driving at. When she did waves of panic began crashing through her.

'Don't be ridiculous! I'm not here because I want to *discuss* anything with you,' she told him. 'I've made my decisions and your opinion on the subject isn't and never was an issue for me. I certainly don't need your financial support.'

Reb didn't mind her disregarding his financial assistance—heck, her family could buy and sell most people ten times over—but if she was carrying his child he'd be damned if he'd have her ride roughshod over his right to express an opinion of how to deal with the situation!

'Now just a—' he started.

'This is my address, in Sydney,' she said, holding out a business card to him.

Reb took the peach business card and scanned it. Apart from her name, embossed in a delicate gold script, it revealed nothing other than her box number at an Eastern Suburbs post office.

'You live at a *post office*?'

She ignored his facetiousness. 'My doctor wants details of any medical problems the baby might inherit from you. I need to know if there's a history of things like asthma or diabetes or…er…congenital birth defects.' Her voice cracked a fraction, but she quickly recovered herself. 'When you get the relevant information you can mail it to me at that address. And *that* will be the end of it.'

At the sight of a huge motorbike speeding into the driveway Amanda-Jayne's heart almost lurched out of her chest. Desperate to avoid being seen here and starting any possible rumours which might hint at Reb Browne and herself having had a relationship, she instantly reached for the ignition key. The noise of the bike interrupted whatever Reb had been saying and when he stepped back to shoot an annoyed look at the rider Amanda-Jayne snapped off the parking brake and flattened the accelerator. The car gave a tricky little slide as she hit the loose gravel at the side of the road at speed, but mercifully, despite her supposed bald tyres, once onto the bitumen she again found traction. A quick look in the rear-view mirror revealed an angry-looking Reb Browne staring after her as a black-clad biker stopped alongside him.

The image was a graphic reminder of exactly who and what the father of her child was, and reassured her she was doing the right thing in excluding him from her child's future. It might have been different if he'd been a lawyer or an accountant or…even just an *ordinary* mechanic. But Bad Boy Browne was a hellraiser from the tips of his biker boots to his unruly raven hair and no child should have to pay for one act of bad judgment on the part of its mother.

CHAPTER TWO

THOUGH the coolness of the marble entrance foyer provided respite from the early evening's heat, it did little to stem the nausea, which had hit Amanda-Jayne at the garage. Feeling that at any moment she might join the ranks of the generations of deceased Vaughans, who peered down at her from the walls, she hurried towards the staircase, desperately swallowing back the acid bile rising in her throat and hoping to reach her bedroom without throwing up.

'There you are!' Amanda-Jayne stifled a groan as her stepmother's gleeful disapproval caught her at the bottom of the stairs. 'Where on earth have you been?'

'Out,' she responded, continuing up the stairs without turning.

'Don't be smart with me, Amanda-Jayne. Have you forgotten we're expected at the mayoral ball in a little over an hour?'

Amanda-Jayne had, but it was a moot point now since it was eminently feasible that within the hour she'd be dead from terminal morning sickness. 'I'm not going, Patricia. I'll call Mayor Bur—'

'What do you mean, you won't be going? You most certainly will be!'

Since dealing with her stepmother could turn her stomach even on its good days Amanda-Jayne had no intention of lingering for a lecture now, so with her mouth firmly shut she continued on up the stairs, dogged by dizziness, nausea and, worst of all, Patricia.

'I expect you to be ready in forty-five minutes. I also expect that you'll show more style in your choice of evening wear than you did when you chose your current attire.'

'Patricia,' she said wearily. 'The only evening wear I'll be putting on are my pyjamas.'

'Now you listen here, Amanda-Jayne… This family has a tradition of being guests of honour at the New Year's ball and I will not tolerate you snubbing your nose at it. You hear me? You always attended when your father was head of this family so don't think you can embarrass me by not going now I hold that position.'

'I don't need to embarrass you, Patricia; Joshua is managing to do that on his own.'

'You leave my son out of this. He's only a child.'

The sheer absurdity of *that* remark couldn't go unchallenged. 'He's eighteen—hardly a child. Although given the way he almost ploughed down an elderly couple outside the post office a few minutes ago then hurled four-letter words at them, the term juvenile delinquent would be pretty accurate.'

'Telling tales again, sis?' Her half-brother's amused voice rose from the foyer.

'Darling, you're home!'

Patricia's singsong delight at her son's appearance was the last straw for Amanda-Jayne's stomach. With one hand sealing her mouth she sprinted down the hall to her room, where she used the other to defy Patricia's, 'Don't you dare lock that door, Amanda-Jayne! I want to speak with you.' Then, with the bedroom swirling around her, she dashed to her private bathroom.

She was dimly aware of her stepmother thumping on the bedroom door, but she had no idea what she was shouting at her. Considering Patricia's vocal-amplification abilities, she could only assume that hearing impairment was a side effect of heaving one's heart out.

Dear God, how much longer would this last?

For over a week now she'd been getting up close and personal with the commode at varying and multiple times each day. *Morning* sickness? Ha! She hoped whatever idiot had named it that had been exiled in disgrace from the

world of medical science and was at this minute eyeballing
Satan!

'My doctor wants details of any medical problems the baby
might inherit from you… When you get the relevant information you can mail it to me… And *that* will be the end
of it.'

For the thousandth time, Reb's mind replayed the scene
at the garage.

'Like hell that'll be the end of it,' he said, rolling the
beer bottle he'd emptied nearly an hour ago between his
palms. 'If I've fathered a kid, Ms I-didn't-need-your-
financial-assistance Vaughan, I'm sure as hell going to contribute more than just a medical report to its future.'

Reb wasn't yet sure what exactly he was going to say or
precisely what demands he was going to lay on Amanda-
Jayne when he fronted up at the Vaughan house tomorrow
morning, but one thing was sure: she wouldn't want to
count on her New Year getting off to the start she'd
planned. He might have been too shell-shocked to entirely
comprehend what she'd said prior to speeding out of the
garage earlier this evening, but he wasn't giving her the
satisfaction of thinking she was calling all the shots for
much longer. First thing tomorrow morning he was going
to be on her doorstep ready to set a few ground rules of
his own and she'd better be ready to listen.

'Hoy, Reb! Since when have you got so antisocial?'

At the wry question, Reb lowered his gaze from the inky
sky and watched the approach of the woman who'd delivered it. Wearing ratty sneakers, cut-off jeans and a skimpy
midriff top, the pint-size blonde looked barely old enough
to be in high school, much less the mother of his two-year-
old goddaughter. It was an illusion that vanished the moment she was close enough for anyone to see her eyes. At
a glance they were a startling green…on closer inspection
they were more jaded than green, making Debbie Jenkins

seem decades older than the twenty-one Reb knew her to be.

It occurred to him that Deb's background was the complete antithesis to Amanda-Jayne Vaughan's. A runaway from a home life that was all too familiar to most of Reb's friends, she'd spent a year in a juvenile detention centre before hooking up with a group of bikers that even he'd regarded as bad news. But in the best traditions of irony she'd got 'lucky' just over three years ago when her loser boyfriend had put her up as collateral in a pub card game and Reb had 'won' her. If she'd been surprised when he'd said he wasn't interested in having her warm his bed, she'd near died of shock when he'd offered her a ride to Vaughan's Landing and a full-time job working in the garage.

Reb had given her a chance and his mate Gunna had given her his heart. Neither man had ever been sorry.

'So how come you're sittin' out here all by your lonesome?' she asked. 'Not like you to be on the fringes of a party.'

'Just needed a bit of time to consider my New Year resolutions.'

She laughed. 'Let me guess, you're givin' up smokin'…*again*.'

Reb grimaced, regretting that the best he could claim in his latest campaign to quit was having cut back and switched to an ultra low tar/nicotine brand.

'Yeah, that too,' he said. 'Maybe this year I'll manage to give them right away, huh?'

'Well, I'm givin' 'em away,' Debbie asserted proudly. 'And I'm doin' it cold turkey. It's time I set Alanna a good example.'

'I wish I could've managed that. Good luck, Deb; take it from me, you're in for a tough time.'

'Mentionin' tough… What's this I hear about Savvy givin' you the slip?'

Reb paused as a means of checking the anger the question reignited. His fifteen-year-old cousin was going to be lucky if he didn't wring her neck first chance he got.

'We had a disagreement about her going to some party tonight,' he said finally. 'As usual she holed up in her bedroom sulking. Then, while I was talking to Aman—er—a customer,' he amended quickly, 'she bolted. I didn't know she wasn't upstairs until about an hour later, after I finished working on Mrs Kelly's FJ.'

'*Bolted?* You mean ran away?'

'No, no,' Reb said quickly, responding to the alarm in Debbie's expression. 'She hasn't taken any of her stuff. Just snuck off for the night. The brat left a note saying ''Gone to party. Don't wait up.'' I'll kick her butt into the middle of next month when I get hold of her,' he promised.

'I'm surprised you just didn't go right out an' haul her butt home.'

'I would've if I'd had the slightest clue where the party was,' Reb said curtly. 'It's because she wouldn't give me any details in the first place that I said she couldn't go. And her friends were predictably close-mouthed when I rang around trying to find out where it was. Her life won't be worth living when I get my hands on her.'

'Can't be too tough on her, Reb,' she said. 'I mean, she's a kid. Didn't you do the same thing at fifteen?'

Reb hadn't. There had been no point in sneaking out or even asking permission to do something or go somewhere when his old man had let him run his own race from the time he'd been able to walk. He hadn't even started school the first time the cops had brought him home after finding him wandering along the highway. When his old man had died, he'd moved in with his uncle, but the then toddling Savannah was such a handful that Bill had relied on Reb's self-sufficiency to extend to taking care of her as well. Trouble was, the teenage Savvy was proving more of a handful than the hyperactive two-year-old version had ever been.

'Fairness isn't high on my priority list right now,' he

grumbled. 'I've got more than enough problems on my plate without all the stunts she's been pulling these last few months.'

'Problems?' Immediate concern wrinkled Debbie's features. 'With the business?'

'No, thank God! That's the one part of my life that's not currently causing me headaches. Although I'll probably jinx myself sayin—' Reb broke off at the sound of Joe Cocker's voice cranked to a volume loud enough to shatter ice at both poles.

Debbie cursed. 'I just told Gunna not to connect those other two amps! We'll have the cops out here shortly.'

'I don't think you have to worry about breaking any noise acts tonight, Deb. Apart from it being New Year's Eve there's not another house for miles.'

'I hope you're right,' she muttered. 'There's at least a dozen guys here who could get busted just on sight.' She grimaced ruefully. 'But then what else is new, right?

'Now c'mon,' she urged, grabbing his arm. 'It's almost time to count in the New Year and I reckon you and me are the only two still sober enough to manage it!'

It was dark when Amanda-Jayne awoke with a stomach that was mercifully settled and now craving food. Rolling over, she looked at the clock and smiled; at 11:50 p.m. on New Year's Eve even the domestic staff wouldn't be around, but more importantly neither would Patricia. Once again she wondered why she'd been cursed with the Cinderella version of a stepmother when other girls she'd known had got ones who would have crawled over crushed glass for them.

She'd been very young when her father married Patricia and any hopes she'd held that, after being motherless for two years, the quality of her life would only be improved by the marriage had been dashed long before its first anniversary. By then she'd been whole-heartedly entrenched in competition with her stepmother for every scrap of her father's affection. Yet youthful enthusiasm was no match for experienced scheming and Patricia had been so adept at concealing her dislike of her stepdaughter from her husband that it was Amanda-Jayne who'd invariably come out looking bad. For all her late father's famed all-seeing business vision, when it came to seeing through his second wife's charade of 'loving stepmother' Andrew Vaughan had been pathetically myopic and insensitive to how lonely and excluded his daughter had come to feel in her own home. The situation had only worsened when Patricia had given birth to Joshua.

On the rare occasions it was deemed convenient for Amanda-Jayne to spend a weekend home from boarding-school, Patricia had made her feel like an outsider. Therefore, as soon as she'd turned eighteen Amanda-Jayne had chosen to move permanently to Sydney, returning to Vaughan's Landing for only brief command visits to please her father. Since his death, she only returned to meet the terms of his will, but all that would change in forty-four months' time. Come her thirtieth birthday, she'd have full legal title and control over the house.

Making her way down the small staff staircase leading from the upper floor to the kitchen, she couldn't suppress the satisfaction she felt at knowing that Patricia knew she was on borrowed time as head of the house. Thanks to Amanda-Jayne's great-grandfather's very un-Victorian sense of equality, his will stated that in all future generations the Vaughan Hill house must pass to the eldest child regardless of sex. So, although the income from the Vaughans' prosperous, century-old horse and cattle stud was to be equally divided between Joshua and herself, Amanda-Jayne was the heir to the family home. A situation which peeved Patricia no end since it granted her stepdaughter the power to exile her to the small cottage at the other side of the property once she assumed full control of her inheritance. In fact if her father hadn't unreasonably stipulated that Amanda-Jayne couldn't take full control until her thirtieth birthday, Patricia would have been 'slumming it' in the much smaller four-bedroom residence right now instead of still playing lady of the manor.

Some people might think it was mean to force Patricia to move to the smaller house, but Amanda-Jayne refused to acknowledge any guilt about what she intended to do. *Considering the way she kicked me into boarding-school,* she thought, *why should I?* By her father's own admission the decision to send her away to school at age ten had been entirely her stepmother's.

'Patricia feels your mother and I were being extremely short-sighted and selfish in deciding to keep you in day school until senior high,' he'd told her the day before she'd been shipped off to Sydney. 'Patricia did two years of an education degree at university so she's better qualified to make this decision than I am. You'll thank her in the end.'

Well, 'the end' was still out of sight in any direction Amanda-Jayne looked, especially since whatever arguments her stepmother had used to convince her husband that she was an 'education expert' must have exceeded their use-by date when it had come time for her son's education. Joshua hadn't started boarding-school until this past year and already Patricia was dropping hints—the largest being the Ferrari Josh had got the day he'd gained his licence—that he wouldn't be returning for his final year and silently daring Amanda-Jayne to challenge her on the subject.

Amanda-Jayne had refused to rise to the bait by demanding to know how much driving a kid could do with only one weekend away from school every four weeks. She'd outgrown playing Patricia's little games; they took more enthusiasm than she could muster for the woman. As for Josh...well, for all that he was spoilt and arrogant, deep down Amanda-Jayne actually *liked* him, and there had been occasions in the past when she'd suspected he felt the same way about her, despite the fact Patricia had made it her life's work to prevent any sibling affection developing between them.

While she wanted to think maturity was the reason she

was now able to handle her stepmother's obvious manipulation and open antagonism without immediately becoming defensive or losing her temper, it was more likely her tolerance stemmed from knowing her visits home were irregular and blissfully short. The exception being this dumb, annual two-week Christmas/New Year family reunion, which her father had so embraced he'd actually made it a condition of his will that the remaining members of his 'loving family' maintain the tradition. Amanda-Jayne might have laughed at the irony of that had she been able to understand *anything* of what her father had been thinking when he'd drawn up his last will and testament.

While she'd fight anyone who said her father hadn't been of sound mind when he'd drawn up the document, her own opinion was that he must have been at least midway through a crate of imported cognac when he'd insisted the family solicitor couldn't pay her monthly allowance until Patricia had verified she'd fulfilled their family obligations. She wondered if her father would be surprised to learn his precious wife had conveniently forgotten to instruct the solicitors to transfer Amanda-Jayne's allowance *every* month since his death?

In the past it had taken no more than a couple of curt phone calls to rectify the problem, but Amanda-Jayne hadn't seen a cent of her trust money for three months. If it wasn't in her account when she got back to Sydney her father and every soul in both heaven and hell would hear the commotion she was going to kick up. Her ex-husband had already cost her the money she'd taken into their marriage; she wasn't about to placidly sit around showing 'good faith' while she got financially routed a second time.

For the life of her she had no idea why her father had tied up her inheritance the way he had. Sometimes she thought it was because he'd had his own doubts on the success of her marriage and had wanted to safeguard her income, but that didn't really make sense since he'd practically hand-picked his son-in-law. Which just went to prove, she thought ruefully, that his judgment in son-in-laws had been every bit as appalling as his taste in second wives.

Opening the refrigerator, Amanda-Jayne studied its contents for several moments before deciding that strawberries and cream along with some non-alcoholic wine from the cellar was as good a way as any to celebrate the New Year solo. No sooner had the self-pitying thought flashed into her head than an inner warmth and the recollection of precisely why she was spending the night at home ousted it.

'Sorry, sweetie,' she whispered, looking down and placing a hand on her still flat belly. 'You're a wonderful surprise… It's just that I'm still getting used to you.'

'You tart! You cheap, good-for-nothing tramp! How dare you humiliate—?'

Amanda-Jayne's first, sleep-clouded thought was that she'd forgotten to switch off her TV. It wasn't until her arm was almost reefed from its socket that it registered the diatribe of abuse was being directed at *her*!

Instantly awake, a startled scream burst from her as her eyes fought the sudden intrusion of light and her body resisted Patricia, who for some reason was trying to drag her from her bed.

'Patricia, stop it!' she demanded.

'Get out!' Patricia shouted. 'Get out *now*!'

'Let me go! Let—'

Though her stepmother released her arm, it was only to snatch the doona and pillows from the bed and hurl them to the floor. 'Get out!' she screeched again. 'Out of bed! And out of this house!'

Amanda-Jayne was only too willing to concede that Patricia had a lot of vices, but drinking wasn't one of them, so she could only conclude that the teetotalling witch had rabies. Except rabies didn't exist in Australia, which meant—

'Mum! Stop!'

As Josh grabbed his mother's wildly flaying arms, survival instincts sent Amanda-Jayne scampering off the far side of the mattress.

On the other side of the bed a worried-looking Joshua was restraining his vermilion-faced mother, but shock was making it hard for Amanda-Jayne's sleep-hazed brain to get any handle on what was going on. In all the years of their mutual animosity Patricia had never done anything this…this *bizarre*. But then again Amanda-Jayne had never imagined so much anger and contempt could radiate from a person's eyes as was being directed at her now.

It was a hatred so intense Patricia was physically shaking from it and it didn't require too much mental effort to work out what had triggered it; somehow her stepmother had discovered she was pregnant.

'How *dare* you humiliate Joshua and me like this?' she berated her. 'How are we supposed to maintain our dignity in this town when you've disgraced the family by…by *bedding* common scum? A loutish, barbaric hoodlum!'

Amanda-Jayne reeled at her words. It was one thing for her to have found out about the baby, but the baby's *father*…! Dear God, how had *that* got out? Yet even as she asked the question she knew. Why should she have thought that Reb Browne was above recounting his sexual conquests and the consequences thereof? Yet the irrational sense of betrayal she felt was a thousand times worse than that which her philandering ex-husband had ever caused her.

Anger at her own naivety, her stepmother and men in general rose up until she tasted its bile. Until—

Hand across her mouth, she flew to the bathroom, slamming the door against Patricia's judgmental words. She wanted to cry. And at the same time wanted to punch something—or better yet *someone who wasn't female and was responsible for getting her into this condition*!

When she re-entered the bedroom fifteen minutes later with an empty but still queasy stomach and a thumping

headache Joshua had left, but her stepmother was still there
and had obviously managed to keep herself busy; all the
wardrobe doors were wide-open and dresser drawers pulled
out and emptied. What clothes weren't tossed on the bed
lay in hateful disarray on the floor.

'I want you packed and out of here within the hour.'

'Fine,' she stated coolly, refusing, *absolutely refusing*, to
give Patricia the satisfaction of seeing her buckle under. 'I
assure you I've no more desire to be here than you have
for me to stay, but…' she paused, more in a bid to maintain
her composure than for emphasis '…I'll leave with a
cheque for the three months' allowance I'm owed.'

'Oh, no, you won't! Your father left me with the responsibility of seeing the high standard of dignity the
Vaughan family has preserved for generations was main-
tained by—'

'Well, then, Patricia, considering your display tonight,
you've let him down badly, haven't you?'

'How dare you accuse *me* of such a thing, after the way
you've disgraced yourself? You've sullied the family name
and reputation—*my* name and reputation!' she added. 'I'm
not going to give you one cent!'

'My father left me that money and—'

'And he gave me the power to decide whether you fill
the requirements to receive it!' Patricia shrieked, whatever
control she might have regained while Amanda-Jayne was
in the bathroom fast dwindling. 'Now I want you out of
my house, immediately. Do you hear me? *Immediately!*
How dare you desecrate my reputation like this,
you…you…?'

'Obviously, your memory is failing since you consider
this *your* house, so I'll be helpful and remind you that tart
and tramp were your nouns of choice earlier. But your opinion means less than nothing to me and—'

'My opinion reflects what any decent person's will be
now it's known you're…you're…having a relationship
with a common criminal!'

As much as she hated to defend the man whose bragging mouth had put her in this situation, she wasn't in the mood to concede her stepmother anything. 'Reb Browne might've had a few juvenile crosses against his name, but he's earning an honest living now. What's more, we aren't "having a relationship".'

All colour drained from Patricia's face. 'Dear Lord! Have you *no* shame? No morals *at all*?'

Since it was a question Amanda-Jayne's own conscience had berated her with all too often of late it was a struggle to keep her voice flippant and cool. 'According to you, apparently not. However, neither do I have my last three months' trust fund allowance. Since *that* is my immediate concern, and I won't leave until I have it, I think it should also be yours.'

It took all of Amanda-Jayne's willpower to remain stony-faced as she crossed the room and opened the door for her stepmother. 'If you'll excuse me, Patricia, I have packing to do and *you* have a very large cheque to write…'

Patricia fled the room muttering unintelligibly; in the wake of her exit, Amanda-Jayne locked the door and then dissolved into tears, uncertain of precisely *why* she was crying, but not able to stop.

Thirteen days later, surrounded by the white-on-white luxury of her harbourside penthouse, she was again fighting tears, but on this occasion she knew they had nothing to do with her pregnancy-erratic hormones and everything to do with her impossibly desperate situation and her inability to find any solution to it.

When she'd driven away from the family home in the pre-dawn hours on January the first, she'd allowed herself to believe that not only was she starting a fresh year but a fresh phase in her life. There had been enormous satisfaction in taking Patricia's cheque and stating that she wouldn't be returning until the day she turned thirty and assumed control of the house.

Her exit line had been intended to remind Patricia that ultimately it would be she who'd be calling all the shots—except the reality was that she'd shot herself in the foot and was rapidly bleeding to death.

'Oh, God,' she whispered, tears dropping onto the letter she held in her hand. 'What am I going to *do*?'

She was a fool. An arrogant, useless, unemployable, nearly three months pregnant fool.

She should have anticipated that Patricia would stop payment on the cheque. Just as she should have known that the fuddy-duddy family solicitors would side with Patricia when she claimed that Amanda-Jayne's pregnancy violated the clause in her father's will stating, '*…if in the opinion of my wife either of my children act in a manner which invites scandal, or in any way damages the good name of the family, their trust allowance is to be suspended for whatever length of time my wife sees fit, up to but not beyond the age where they are eligible to gain full control of their individual trusts.*'

Amanda-Jayne tried to muffle the half sob, half laugh which broke from her as she gazed out at her multi-million-dollar view of the Opera House and Sydney Harbour Bridge. She was the heir to a fortune, with one of the most expensive roofs imaginable over her head, and she'd be lucky to be able to pay her next electricity bill, much less pay the sum overdue on the lease agreement for her car. Her credit cards were already maxed out and unless she could find a way to keep up the cost of her private health insurance she was going to be facing an enormous medical bill in just over six months' time.

The idea of having her baby under the public heath scheme terrified her, not because she didn't believe it was more than adequate, but because she wanted her own ob-gyn. Dr Geermaine knew her complicated medical history, he knew how important this pregnancy was to her. *He was the one who'd said it may well be her only chance at motherhood.* Maybe if she explained her predicament when she went to deliver the medical records Reb Browne had sent he'd agree to keep her on as a private patient.

After all, it's not as if I'm a welfare case, she thought with bitter irony, tossing the letter of demand onto the desk already scattered with a host of other bills with 'URGENT ATTENTION REQUIRED' stamped in red. *Oh, no! I'm too 'asset-rich' to qualify for any social security!*

After days of hanging out at the unemployment office and attending countless interviews, which had only high-lighted her total lack of employment skills, she'd today swallowed every last vestige of her pride and made an appointment at the local social security office. It had turned out to be the most humiliating and humbling experience of her entire life. It had never occurred to her not to dress well for what in her mind was a business appointment, but the way her expensive clothes had contrasted against those of most of the other welfare applicants had consumed her with guilt. Had she been able to think of *any* other way to solve her immediate cash problem, she'd have walked straight back out of the office the moment she arrived. Which would have at least saved her two and a half wasted hours and achieved the same results.

After presenting the required copy of her tax return from the previous year, bank statements and evidence of all stock and property in her name, they had been shoved back at her by a teenage clerk with too much make-up and no manners.

'Ms Vaughan, I can understand how someone like you would be ignorant of the social security system,' she'd said, making little effort to hide her amusement. 'But the Government isn't in the habit of giving money to people who clearly don't need it.'

'But I *do* need it,' Amanda-Jayne had protested, swallowing even more pride by admitting, 'I've got bills coming out of my ears—'

'Then I suggest you do what the rest of us do—*get a job.*'

'I've tried! For your information there's an unemployment problem in this country.'

'I can assure you, Ms Vaughan, I'm in a better position than you are to know about that. However, government assistance is only granted on the basis of a means test. It's not given out to wealthy women with more assets than brains.'

'Excuse me!'

'Gladly,' the girl quipped. 'Next, please!'

When Amanda-Jayne had demanded to see a supervisor, she'd had to wait twenty minutes for a harried-looking man in his late thirties. After complaining firstly about his junior clerk's attitude and then pleading her case, the man had quickly scanned the documents she'd brought, then slid them back in the folder and grinned at her. 'Lucky you, Ms Vaughan. Stop wasting both our time.'

It had taken every bit of her resolve not to dissolve into tears on the spot, but in the wake of the letter of demand from the car dealership they now flowed freely, blurring her scenic view until the harbour seemed to swallow up everything—everything except her fears. What was—?

She jumped as her front door reverberated from a series of loud thumps. Followed by an incessant ring on her doorbell.

'Let me in, A.J.! I know you're there!'

Reb Browne.

Her heart had dropped into her shoes, but all her brain could assimilate was that after the day from hell she really should have been expecting that the devil himself would pay her a visit.

CHAPTER THREE

REB hastily 'pulled his punch' when the door, towards which his fist was again heading, was reefed open and Amanda-Jayne stepped into its path.

'How on earth did you get in here?'

Her tone implied people wearing jeans and carrying leather jackets and bike helmets were usually shot on sight by the doorman, but what gave Reb pause was her face. There was no question she was every bit as beautiful as he remembered, but despite her cool, controlled expression and regal poise there was also no question she'd been *crying*. A lot.

For some reason the notion of Amanda-Jayne Vaughan crying was as incongruous as it was disturbing and it took him several seconds to refocus on what she was saying.

'...security block. Now how did you get my address and who let you in?'

'The guy on the door seemed to think this qualified as a pass key.' Grinning, he handed her the business card she'd previously given him. 'It was the *back* that impressed him most,' he added as she frowned at the card.

'"Hoping to hear from you soon,"' she read, the pitch and disbelief in her voice rising with each word. '"Drop in and surprise me. A.J.!" This isn't my writing!'

'Lucky for me, the doorman didn't know that,' Reb said, stepping around her to stroll into the centre of her living room.

'Mmm, nice view you've got here. Although I don't go much on this bleached decor—'

'How did you get my address?' she demanded. '*I* didn't give it to you.'

'No, and neither would your mother, so—'

'*Step*mother.'

The force of her correction was telling. 'Ah,' he said sagely, 'so that's the way the wind blows. Well, that's something we have in common; I wasn't real taken with the woman either.'

'I'm not interested in your opinion of Patricia,' she said, her eyes flashing with rage. 'I asked how you found out where I lived.'

'Just a matter of posting off those medical records you wanted and waiting until you went to the post office to pick them up.'

'You've been *following* me?'

'Not personally. But if you ever need a good P.I. let me know.'

'How dare you? You have no right to invade my privacy that way.'

'Sweetheart, you're carrying *my* child, which as far as I'm concerned gives me a whole heap of rights. So as of right now you can forget any ideas you've got about cutting me out of its life. You mightn't have much of an opinion of me or my gene pool, but you're way off base if you think I'm going to walk away from my own flesh and blood.'

Amanda-Jayne felt herself teetering on the brink of hysteria and immediately her stomach started acting up again. Taking a steadying breath, she tried to assimilate the fact that Reb Browne had tracked her down and was actually in her living room. *Nothing* was working out as she'd envisaged; all her hopes of an uncomplicated pregnancy were going from bad to disastrous. Her morning sickness was never-ending, all the money she'd expected to have she *didn't* and the father she'd counted on fading into the background *hadn't*. This wasn't the way things were supposed to go! It was just supposed to be her, her baby and a future filled with happiness. Instead...instead... *Oh, God,* she prayed, *please don't let me start crying in front of him.*

Reb watched as a dozen emotions rushed across her pale face, but he couldn't guess at what she was thinking. Still, there was no doubt his announcement had shaken her up, but since that had been his intention it irked him that he was now feeling guilty about it. He'd meant what he said; no way was he going to be shut out of his kid's life.

Unnerved by her ongoing silence and suspecting she was hoping it would either force him to speak first or simply give up and walk out, he made a production of tossing his jacket and helmet onto her well-stuffed sofa then dropping down beside them.

Amanda-Jayne opened her mouth to demand that he leave, but before she could form the words her common sense suddenly started jumping up and down and yelling, *Think, you idiot! He's here because he wants to contribute to the baby's upkeep… And right now you need money. Even if it is his!*

That the man who was currently draped over her sofa like a model in a jeans commercial was the answer to her prayers didn't sit at all well with her; in fact it further agitated her already distressed stomach. However, the reality was she wasn't in any position to pander to her pride. She was up to her eyeballs in bills and facing countless more in the next few months. Swallowing the taste of bile along with a chunk of her self-esteem, Amanda-Jayne forced herself to speak calmly and civilly.

'Am I to understand it,' she said, 'that you hired a private investigator to follow me simply because you're determined to contribute to the baby's upbringing?'

'I think I made that more than clear to you when you came to see me. And you,' he said, 'made a point of throwing the offer back in my face then skipping town.'

'I…er…didn't want to be responsible for placing you under a financial strain.' It was a lie and the smile on his handsome face told her he knew it.

'Very considerate of you, but I think it's best if you let me worry about my finances and you take care of your own.'

If she hadn't felt so ill she'd have laughed at the irony of his comment, but all she wanted to do was get rid of him before she humiliated herself and lost the contents of her stomach.

'Very well, then,' she said briskly. 'Since you're so insistent and have gone to such extreme lengths to find me and pursue the matter, I'm prepared to accept your financial assistance. I'll speak to my solicitor tomorrow and have him draw up the necessary paperwork.'

'Oh, that won't be necessary; I've already got *my* solicitor taking care of that,' he said.

The one-upmanship in his voice tempted her to say she hadn't realised criminal lawyers handled maintenance cases, but she decided to quit while she was ahead for the first time in weeks. 'In that case, I'll give you the address of mine.'

She'd just started to cross to her desk when he mentioned the monthly sum he considered reasonable and she nearly staggered with surprise. It wasn't a fortune, but it was far more than she'd have been getting even if she'd qualified for social security. While she had no idea what garage proprietors made, she doubted Reb would have very much left for himself once he'd paid out that large a sum to her. Given her own recent experience of being cash-poor, she didn't feel comfortable putting anyone else in that position; not even him.

'Er...that's very generous,' she said, almost choking on the desire to say, I'll take it! 'But are you sure you can afford that much?'

'I thought we agreed I'd worry about my finances and you'd worry about yours?'

Well, so much for trying to be considerate and reasonable! Stung by his cavalier attitude, she sent him her frostiest glare then hurriedly scribbled down the details of her solicitor. Returning to where he lounged on her sofa, she held the piece of paper out to him at arm's length. 'Here. I don't think we have anything more to discuss. I'll accept your offer as it stands.'

'I'm afraid there's a condition to my offer...'

Amanda-Jayne swallowed hard. 'What?'

'You have to marry me to get it.'

At his deadly serious expression Amanda-Jayne's heart lurched into her throat. 'Marr—oh, God, I'm going to be sick!'

By the time Reb recovered from the shock of her words and the sight of her racing across the room with a hand clamped over her mouth, Amanda-Jayne had locked herself in what he presumed was the bathroom. Her initial responses to his enquiries as to whether there was anything he could do were merely a series of worrying retches, gags and heart-wrenching whimpers and he was considerably relieved when these eventually progressed to curses, demands that he get out and accusations of, 'This is all your fault!'

It was almost an hour before she re-emerged wearing what Savvy referred to as a slip-dress—a plain spaghetti-strapped navy shift that brushed her ankles above feet that were bare and sporting cherry-coloured toenails.

She shot Reb a lethal glare. 'I thought I told you to get out?'

'You did. Several times. But I never walk away from a card game when I have all the trumps.'

'The only thing you have,' she fired back, 'are delusions of grandeur or a serious drug problem! Why on earth would I want to marry you for a measly monthly sum like you offered? Potentially I'm worth more than you can even dream about.'

'That might be so. But right now,' he said, strolling to her desk and picking up a fistful of the bills littering it, 'your *potential* worth is about as useful to you as last week's TV guide.'

She raced to snatch the papers from his hand. 'How dare

you snoop through my personal papers? Just because I'm a bit behind—'

'Cut the act, A.J.,' he said tersely. 'We both know you're in debt up to your pretty little ears and that your trust fund has been frozen.'

Even as embarrassment warred with anger in her face, Reb could practically hear the gears in her head rotating as she fought to engage her brain. He knew the instant she had by the flash of triumph in her whisky-brown eyes.

'Not that it's any of your business,' she said haughtily, 'but I happen to be in the process of negotiating the sale of this penthouse. I can assure you that once that's finalised money will be the least of my problems.'

Reb grinned. 'Rubbish. The money for this place was advanced to you from your trust after your divorce, but with the condition that you can't sell it and gain the use of the funds until such time as your inheritance is released to you. According to my sources that's three years down the track.'

Amanda-Jayne clenched her fists and concentrated on not punching him. Never in her entire life had she wanted to hit someone as much as she did Reb Browne. The problem was he was absolutely right. She'd weighed up all her money-raising options and every one was terminally an-orexic. Any way she looked, this odious, arrogant hellraiser was her and her baby's only immediate source of income.

'Well?' he prompted, making no attempt to conceal a smart-alec grin. 'What's your answer?'

'I hate you.'

'I'm not looking for a love match.'

'What exactly *are* you looking for?'

'Stability for my child.'

It was a noble sentiment, but Reb Browne didn't strike her as the noble type. Then again, she'd recently discovered neither was she… When she'd first realised the extent of her money problems she'd intended filing a lawsuit against Patricia as a means of forcing her to release the money she was owed; all that had stopped her was learning the family solicitors would side with Patricia and that such an action by her would be deemed as bringing the Vaughan name into disrepute, thus contravening her father's wishes anyway. She was in a position where she was going to be damned if she did, damned if she didn't and, Lord help her, *damned well going to have to marry Reb Browne*!

Surely a person was supposed to be dead before having to endure hell? Then again, hadn't she'd already experienced it once in this lifetime? She'd managed to survive seven years in one bad marriage; what was a further measly three in another one? she reasoned.

Besides, in a few months the baby would provide her with all the happiness she'd ever need. It was the baby she had to think of; even though the very idea of being Mrs Browne filled her with an almost electric dread there was simply no other solution. *Unless, of course, I hyphenate my name to Vaughan-Browne!* Finding a glimmer of light in her black humour, she turned to the man whose presence seemed to shrink her spacious apartment to phone-booth proportions. She breathed deeply before saying, 'I'll accept your condition, but I have one of my own... If we marry I want to keep my maiden name.'

Reb told himself the sigh he expelled came from impatience, not relief, but he knew he was lying. His biggest concern had been that she'd refuse to marry him, leaving him next to no legal rights over the baby, and with his family history and her wealthy background he needed as much legal leverage as he could get. Traditionally the women who bore children to the Browne men invariably lacked maternal instincts; his own mother had shot through when he was only ten and Savvy's hadn't stuck around even that long. Neither woman had cared enough to take her kids with her, but if they had, in the absence of a marriage certificate in both cases, there would have been little chance of either his father or uncle getting custody.

Reb might well be the first male Browne to produce a child in wedlock for three generations, but his proposal

wasn't motivated from a moral or social angle, purely a
legal one. He knew that when Amanda-Jayne decided to
call it quits, unlike his mother and aunt, she'd be the type
to take her child with her, if only because she had the
money to do it. He also knew that he couldn't match it with
the Vaughans in an expensive, drawn-out custody battle.
But he sure as hell wasn't going to be shoved entirely from
his child's life and marriage would prevent that happening.

'You can call yourself anything you like,' he said,
snatching up his helmet and jacket. 'I'll be here at nine
tomorrow morning so we can go get a marriage licence.
Once we've done that we'll be heading for Vaughan's
Landing; I've only got the bike so pack light. You can
arrange to have the rest of your stuff sent—'

'What do you mean we'll be heading to Vaughan's
Landing? I'm not going back there! Why would I?'

'We're getting married, remember?'

'As if I could forget! But there's no reason we can't live
here.'

'In case it's slipped your mind, I have a business there
and I'm not about to commute three plus hours twice a
day.'

As insane as it seemed, it wasn't until that moment that
Amanda-Jayne's brain actually grasped what being married
to Reb Browne would mean. Unlike Anthony he wouldn't
be gone for months at a time on business trips; this man
would be in her life every day and, God forbid, possibly
her bed every night! The realisation threw her breathing
pattern into complete disarray, but desperation kept her
mind ticking over for a solution. She almost cheered with
glee as inspiration struck. 'I know!' she said. 'You could
stay in Vaughan's Landing during the week and just come
here on weekends.'

'You mean sleep over on Friday and Saturday nights…'
he said, with a considering expression.

She nodded eagerly. 'Or even just Saturdays! No point
making a long drive after a tough week at—'

'Forget it, sunshine,' he said, cynical amusement in his tone and eyes. 'Like it or lump it, the only people who are going to know this isn't a fair dinkum marriage are you and me.'

'Oh. I see.'

'Do you?' His amused dark-eyed gaze sent heat rushing through her body, but Amanda-Jayne flatly refused to voice the question foremost in her mind.

'Of course,' she said. 'You want our marriage to appear normal at a public level. Very well,' she agreed, before he could take exception to her insinuation that it wasn't going to be normal on a personal level. 'But where in Vaughan's Landing will we live?'

'Where I currently live.' A wry smile tugged at his mouth. 'You should feel almost at home—technically it's a penthouse too.'

'*You* have a penthouse?'

'*Technically*… I live in a flat above the garage.'

She sank onto the arm of the sofa as her mind threw up a picture of the art deco-style cream-painted building on the outskirts of town between the flood plains and the industrial estate. 'Oh, my God…'

Reb hadn't come here intending to blackmail her into marriage—indeed he hadn't even known he was going to make such a condition until he'd heard himself say the words—but any thoughts of revoking them vanished when she dropped her head into her hands as if he'd condemned her to a death sentence rather than saved her financial butt. It wasn't that he'd expected or even wanted her gratitude, but he resented the fact she had the ability to make him dissatisfied with a lifestyle which had suited him just fine until now.

Glancing around the sleek, modern apartment with its multi-million-dollar price tag, he saw nothing that reflected the passion Amanda-Jayne had revealed in his arms that night over two months ago. Nor did he see her being overwhelmed by the functional but uninspired decor of his own two-bedroom abode. Although the idea of how she'd react to both that and Savvy appealed to his warped sense of humour. Still, now wasn't the time to dwell on such things; he wanted to get this sorted out as quickly as possible, while he held all the aces. If she started thinking too hard about ways out of her problems which would spare her marrying him, Reb was back to square one regarding his rights to the baby.

'Make a list of all your outstanding bills; I'll fix them up tomorrow, before we leave.'

Her head came up in amazement. '*All* of them? Even the car?'

'*You mean you owe money on the car too?*'

Amanda-Jayne swallowed at his pained disbelief and tried not to sound intimidated by it. 'You mean your investigator didn't tell you that because I haven't had any income for three months I got behind on the monthly paym—?'

'How much?'

'It's not a lot considering that—'

'How much?' he repeated tightly, flinching when she answered.

'Well, if you think I'm forking out that much for a car that's as much use in a rural area as a screen door on a sub, you can forget it,' he told her. 'However, I'll investigate paying it out and selling—'

'*But I'll need that car!*'

'Why?'

She looked at him as if he were brain-dead. 'To get around in of course. I'll need to go to doctor's appointments and…and shopping—'

'You're hardly in a financial position to be planning too many shopping expeditions,' he said dryly. 'And, surprising as this may be to you, a luxury sports car *isn't* essential for getting to and from the doctor's. Sell it and I'll find you a more practical and economical mode of—'

'B-b-but that car means the world to me!'

'Why?'

'Why?' she echoed, trying to think of a reason that was more logical than the truth.

'Yeah. It's not like you have a mechanical appreciation of it. You don't even know when the tyres are bald.'

'Well…because it's *mine*. It's the first car I've bought—'

'No, you haven't bought it,' he corrected. 'You've got it on hire purchase at some ridiculous interest rate—*which I doubt you even bothered to look at*—and as a result unless you can come up with the money to pay it out by the end of the week it's going to be repossessed!' he said cruelly.

'There's no way I'm going to finance a car that's totally impractical for what it's going to be required for,' he told her. 'Which means if you want to keep it *you'll* have to find a way to pay for it—'

'Fine! I will!'

'By tomorrow. I'll see myself out,' he said, praying she was bluffing about paying off the car. If she could come up with the cash required to keep it, then she also had a means to get out of her current difficulties without having to marry him. 'You know, A.J., you're really going to have to brush up on the quaint manners of the working class once we're married… We not only walk visitors to the door, we offer them refreshments.'

For a moment she looked indignant enough to explode. Then she did. 'Oh, go to hell! Given a choice I wouldn't offer you the time of day.'

'I know.' He grinned at her from the doorway. 'Which is why it was a real surprise when you were so giving of body!'

Reb didn't know what crashed against the door as he was closing it, but from the sound of it smashing it could've caused him a nasty concussion; maybe he ought to keep his helmet on and the visor down when he picked her up in the morning.

It took Amanda-Jayne several hours to calm down and get her brain working with any degree of clarity, but once she started to analyse her predicament things didn't appear quite so bleak; indeed by midnight, when she returned from the apartment directly below her, she was feeling decidedly smug.

Ever since she'd moved here her downstairs neighbour, Oscar Cavenor, had been trying to coerce her into letting him sublet her penthouse to the overseas movie stars he regularly had to find accommodation for while they were in Sydney shooting movies. In the past she'd turned him down cold, but tonight she'd made a deal with him that for the amount of the outstanding sum on her car he could sublet her fully furnished penthouse for twelve months and keep all the revenue. Fiscally she knew she could have done better, but because of the trust she wasn't allowed to turn a profit on the apartment for three years, which was why she couldn't sell it. But Oscar's greed and his self-interest had in itself been a guarantee he'd not ask why she was so desperate for money and for that she was grateful; at least she hadn't had to lie.

She knew few people would understand her obsession with the car, but she didn't care; to her the convertible was a symbol of freedom. She'd walked into the car dealership and bought it the day she'd left Anthony and it represented her finally taking complete control of her life. It was the first time she'd had a vehicle which wasn't chosen, paid for and registered to either a father determined to keep control over her life, or a husband who could sell it out from under her once he'd depleted all the assets she'd brought into their marriage. Losing that car would have signified her ultimate failure in a way nothing else could have and thanks to Patricia's bitchiness that had very nearly happened. Mercifully, though, as of tonight Amanda-Jayne had started to fight for what she wanted and had succeeded in regaining a partial hold on her dream of absolute independence.

While selling the car—which thanks to Oscar she'd own

outright tomorrow morning—would give her sufficient cash to tell Reb Browne what he could do with his marriage proposal, it wouldn't bring enough money to maintain her and the baby for the three years until she got her inheritance. But she had come up with a plan to circumvent that problem…

The rumours of the supposed 'imminent betrothal' between 'Bad Boy Browne' and the town's so-called princess would spread through Vaughan's Landing at the speed of light. Once Patricia heard them she'd be so horrified by the notion she'd not only order Amanda-Jayne's trust money to be released, but would bend over backwards to convince her stepdaughter to leave town.

'Like I'll need convincing!' she chuckled, switching off her bedside lamp and sliding beneath her sheets. As bizarre as Reb Browne's 'condition' had seemed mere hours ago, it was going to turn out to be the best thing that could have happened to her.

CHAPTER FOUR

REB sat down at the first vacant table in the truck stop which years ago had become his halfway stopping point on the trip between Sydney and Vaughan's Landing. Turning his head, he stared outside at the midnight-blue convertible parked beside his bike, his mind still obsessing over the same issue it had been all day... *Was Amanda-Jayne even more shallow than he'd assumed, or did her articulate, well-bred mannerisms conceal a mind that struggled to grasp the obvious?*

This morning, when she'd insisted they stop at a bank before going to the registry of Births, Deaths and Marriages for a licence, he'd assumed she'd been withdrawing whatever limited cash she still had; instead she'd walked out with a cheque made out to the firm about to repossess her car. Not just a cheque to clear the overdue payments, but one big enough to clear the entire outstanding balance. Wearing an ear-to-ear grin, she'd waved it in Reb's face, telling him a friend she'd lent money to had finally been able to repay her.

Reb didn't buy the story and was convinced she'd hit up one of her rich mates for a loan, but his theory didn't invalidate the cheque nor the fact she'd managed to outmanoeuvre him. All night the realist in him had warned that the smug satisfaction he'd been feeling could turn out to be premature, because the prospect of marrying someone like him would spur a woman of Amanda-Jayne's ilk to any lengths to avoid it, so he couldn't claim to have been caught totally unaware. Still, he'd been furious at being back at square one and after 'congratulating' her on the fortuitous stroke of luck he'd stormed out of the bank deciding it was time he saw a lawyer.

But if he hadn't been surprised by the cheque he sure as hell had been when she'd run out of the bank behind him and, with wide-eyed alarm, declared, *'But of course I'm still going to marry you! I couldn't possibly sell my car!'*

Only sheer amazement had prevented Reb from telling her she was crazy. The cheque would have not only cleared her debts and enabled her to buy a sound, used car, but still left sufficient change to adequately support herself even if he hadn't been prepared to contribute to the expenses her pregnancy incurred and the baby's future upkeep. While her decision suited his agenda, he was damned if he could understand it. He'd railroaded her into a situation which had initially had her tossing her stomach and yet when an escape route had presented itself she'd ignored it for the sake of a *car*.

He looked away from the window and the sleek sports car beyond to see his 'fiancée' crossing from the ladies' bathroom towards his table. He couldn't help admiring the soft sensuality her body radiated in motion and there was as yet no way an observer would suspect she was pregnant. Yet considering her behaviour this morning Reb could only assume that either pregnancy seriously impaired a woman's powers of logical thinking or Amanda-Jayne was the shallowest person he'd ever met.

She was also, he noted, a peculiar shade of green as she slid into the chair opposite him. 'Are you okay?'

'No, but I'm hoping some dry toast and tea will settle things.' At his frown she added, 'Morning sickness. Unfortunately, *my* stomach doesn't comprehend time and goes feral at will.' She sighed. 'Obviously I'm not one of those women who glow during pregnancy. Lately I've spent more time looking down toilets than a plumber.'

Her wry humour caught him off guard and he actually had to fight back a grin. It was one thing to lust after her body and to marry her to gain some leverage when the baby was born, but the last thing he wanted was for her to think she could push any of his buttons, that his interest in her went beyond the fact she was carrying his child. *It didn't*.

During the drive from Sydney Amanda-Jayne had struggled to keep her eyes from wandering to the rear-view mirror and the motorcyclist who'd cruised directly behind, but if she'd been burningly aware of him then it was nothing compared to the effect he had on her with only a small café table separating them. In fact she couldn't be positive whether the churning in her stomach *was* actually morning sickness or a nervous reaction to the fact she was going to be living under the same roof as Reb Browne for what might turn out to be as long as a *week* if Patricia decided to prove stubborn.

Still, even as she ruefully accepted she'd displayed the morals of an alley cat in spending a night with Reb Browne, there was no question she'd chosen a good-looking 'tom' with whom to cavort. But then she always did. Anthony had been as drop-dead handsome as he had been unfaithful to her. Not that Anthony's blond, pretty-boy looks and gym-maintained sub-six-foot frame had the gut-heating impact of Reb's blue-collar muscle tone and gypsy dark looks.

'How tall are you?' Reb looked as surprised by her blurted question as she was. 'I…er…was just, you know, wondering how tall the baby might be,' she lied.

'Six-three.'

For want of any sort of intelligent response she nodded then gave her attention to pouring her tea as if it required the concentration of micro-surgery, all the time constantly aware that the dark gaze of the man opposite was focused exclusively on her.

'All the Brownes are tall. Even the females. Savvy is five-ten and she's only fifteen.'

Curiosity stilled her hands, but she managed to stop herself from looking up. 'Savvy?' she muttered vaguely.

'My cousin.'

'Oh.'

Once her cup was finally filled and she'd stirred in milk and sugar, it occurred to her that the only way she'd be able to drink her tea and avoid lifting her head would be if she requested a straw. Since that was beyond ludicrous, she schooled her face to innocence and mentally braced herself for yet another of the penetrating stares Reb had been giving her ever since she'd left the bank. There was no doubt he was curious about where the money had come from, but there was no way he could possibly know of her plans to renege on their wedding. Perhaps if she started a conversation around their supposed wedding she could distract Reb from suspicions he might have.

Lifting her head to find his eyes studying her from behind his coffee cup, she gave an easy smile and picked up her cup. A swallow later she breathed a sigh of relief when her stomach didn't immediately revolt. Still the dark eyes studied her, permeating an excited tension within her and an external silence she was helpless to leave alone.

'I couldn't believe it when it turned out we were both born on the same day,' she said. 'I mean, who'd have credited us both being inflicted with having been born on April Fool's Day? Weird, huh?'

Reb shrugged. 'I'd have said that under the circumstances it wasn't so much weird as poetic justice.'

'Oh, come now. Even the clerk at the registry was surprised.'

'Only because of your reaction,' Reb said dryly. 'You'd just claimed we'd known each other for years and then you go and act all amazed to discover we share the same birthday. *Most people applying for marriage licences know when each other's birthdays fall.*'

'Well, I couldn't help it,' she protested. 'You might have warned me your birthday was April the first.'

'It never occurred to me it would be necessary. I was as surprised as you were, but *unlike you* I didn't dance about singing, "Isn't that just too, too amazing?" in that snobby, gushing tone of yours.'

'Gushing? *Excuse me*, but I'll I have you know I've never *gushed* in my life. My stepmother gushes; I don't.'

'Does that mean you admit to being a snob?'

She knew he expected her to deny it. 'Of course I'm a snob. My father spent a fortune sending me to expensive schools and deportment and elocution classes that mastered in snobbery. In fact,' she said proudly, 'I have *scads* of certificates to *prove* I'm a snob. But for your information snobbery and…er…*gushery*—if there is such a word— aren't necessarily inter-dependent.'

'Gee, it's true what they say…you *do* learn something new every day.' The amusement in his eyes was enough to tell her he was deliberately trying to irritate her with his facetiousness so she forced herself to ignore it.

'Well, no matter what you say, I think it's an uncanny coincidence that we were both born on the same day at the same hospital. Especially when you consider my mother was only at the local hospital because I arrived four weeks early.'

'What makes you think we were born in the same hospital?'

'Well, the bit of your birth certificate I saw stated you were born in Vaughan's Landing… You mean your mother had you at *home*?' She shook her head wistfully. 'Natural childbirth might be regarded as *the* truly maternal thing to do, but I have to be honest, I'm not sure I'll be able to handle it without pain-killers and knowing there are a dozen doctors and midwives surrounding me.'

His laugh was brittle. 'I was born in a tent at a rain-sodden rock concert just outside of town. As for pain-killers, according to the old man my mother was so far off her face on illegal drugs she didn't even know she'd given birth until he told her the next day.'

Amanda-Jayne was shocked beyond a verbal response.

'So frankly, A.J., I don't care whether you elect to have natural childbirth or every *legal* drug known to man, but you better understand right now that, no matter how big a medical team you have during the delivery, when the time comes for you to have *our* baby *I'm going to be there.*'

She was still too aghast by the circumstances of his birth and his cavalier attitude towards it to respond to his comment. Their lives had been so completely different from the moment they'd each entered the world that if she hadn't already been planning to back out of their marriage his revelation would have prompted her to do so. As she reached for her toast, she acknowledged that apart from sharing the same well-ridiculed birthday they had absolutely *nothing* in common.

'You look like hell. Are you going to be all right to drive?' Reb asked fifteen minutes later as she climbed behind the wheel of her car, hoping the fresh air would placate her restless stomach. The toast and tea hadn't been such a great idea after all.

Though an automatic assurance rose to her lips, something in his expression drew the truth from her. 'I'm not sure.' She gave a rueful half-smile. 'I can never be certain if I'm going to be sick until I am. But I don't feel as dizzy as I did driving up here.'

'Dizzy! *You were feeling dizzy and you didn't pull over?*'

'Not pass-out dizzy, just queasy dizzy,' she said, but her explanation only seemed to intensify his frown. 'It only hit me about a kilometre before we got here and I knew I'd make it an—'

He reefed her door open. 'Bloody hell… Get out!'

'Wha—why?'

'Because there's no way I'm letting you get behind the wheel again, possibly endangering your life and anyone else's driving near you, if you black out.'

'Oh, for heaven's sake! I wasn't going to *black out* before. And I'm not going to now. I just told you, I'm not feeling dizzy any more.'

'I'm not interested in debating this with you A.J.… C'mon, *out.*'

'If you think for one minute I'm going to cause a scene

by arriving in town on *that*,' she said, indicating his bike, 'you're out of your mind. I'd like to attract as little attention as possible.'

Reb said wryly, 'Considering the entire town already knows you're carrying my child, that's shutting the gate after the horse has bolted, don't you think?'

'Probably, but I still intend to try and maintain some level of decorum despite the damage you've already caused by bragging about your sexual prowess.'

'You think *I'm* responsible for broadcasting that we're expecting a child?'

'It certainly wasn't *me*! I had no intention of telling *anyone*. Not even—'

'Not even me,' Reb inserted, his expression knowing.

Amanda-Jayne sidestepped the accusation. 'Well, if *you* didn't tell anybody, how did it get all around town, hmm?'

'The usual grapevine, which in this instance had its roots in my cousin overhearing us talking at the garage. Unfortunately she's like most women and couldn't resist sharing what she'd heard with her girlfriends.'

'Pity she wasn't raised to keep her nose out of other people's business.'

'Considering your current circumstances you're hardly in a position to be judgmental of anyone else's upbringing. I doubt too many of the town's mothers are holding you up as a role model to their daughters these days.'

The verbal slap stung for the simple fact that Amanda-Jayne hadn't intended her comment to be anything more than a rueful observation. But as she mentally replayed her words she realised they had smacked of social and moral superiority.

'I didn't mean that the way it sounded,' she said, in lieu of offering an apology. 'I just wish we could have kept this between ourselves.'

'No, you wanted to keep me right out of it,' he countered hotly. 'But because your ivory-towered life got all screwed up that wasn't possible, so now you're prepared to bite the

bullet, endure a stopgap marriage to me until you can collect your inheritance and go back to your semi-regal lifestyle.

'Don't try and deny it A.J.,' he said, forestalling her intended lie. 'I'm not a fool. But understand this… As far as
I'm concerned the fact this marriage is a sham *is* going to
be kept between ourselves. Everyone from my cousin to
your dragon of a stepmother thinks this is a love match and
you're going—'

'Don't be ridiculous! No one in their right mind is going
to believe *that*. For starters I'm hardly ever in Vaughan's
Landing and—'

'They believe it all right, because I've made it a point
to let people know we've been meeting in Sydney for six
months, but were keeping things quiet until your divorce
was final.'

'How dare you slander me that way?'

'You'd have felt better having everyone know we only
shared a one-night stand?'

Reb still didn't know if he'd been trying to protect
Amanda-Jayne's reputation or trying to avoid looking a
fool himself when he'd automatically blurted that lie to his
very curious cousin, but he did know he hadn't expected
to complicate it by insisting they get married.

'Of course I didn't say that we were going to get married,' he said. 'But at least now it's not going to look like
the cold-blooded arrangement it is. People will assume that
since you were pregnant we decided that getting married
was the right thing to do.'

'So what you're saying is that when we're with other
people I'm supposed to fawn over you like some lovesick
groupie?'

The mental image of this cool, sophisticated woman
draping herself over him in public made him grin. 'Not if
you want to be convincing. That kind of behaviour would
be too at odds with your trademark ice-princess routine, but
you will have to stop flinching every time I touch you. And

while the odd adoring look would probably be too much for your acting abilities to cope with maybe you could practise smiling at me every now and then.'

Amanda-Jayne, deciding it was better to let him think she was resigned to her fate, heaved a sigh. 'Okay, I guess you're right. It probably is best if no one knows the truth except us. However, get this straight, Reb Browne... Marriage certificate or not, *I will not be sleeping with you.* This marriage will be real only in front of others so if you don't have two bedrooms in your apartment you'd better like sleeping on the sofa.'

'The apartment has two bedrooms.'

'Good.'

'Fine. Well, now that's settled, get out of the car so—'

'I told you, I am not getting on that bike!'

'And I told you,' he said easily, snatching the keys from the ignition, 'that I'm not letting you drive when you're feeling crook. So shift your cute butt into the passenger seat while I go see the mechanic about leaving the bike here for a day or two.'

Before Amanda-Jayne could utter a word, he pocketed the keys and swaggered off to where two overall-clad men were bent over the engine of a car.

'You lying, conniving rat! You told me there were two bedrooms!'

'There are two bedrooms. Mine and Savvy's.'

'Precisely! And you know as well as I do she's not going to let me share hers.'

'Lucky for you I will, huh?'

Amanda-Jayne eyed the turn-of-the-century oak double bed with disdain. 'It was one thing not to mention your cousin lived with you, Reb, but if you think you can trick me into sleeping with you you're in for a rude sho—' She gasped as Reb snaked out an arm and hauled her against him.

'For God's sake, keep your voice down,' he said. 'You agreed to act like we're an ordinary engaged couple.'

'And *you* agreed we'd have separate bedrooms!'

'No, I didn't. You said if the apartment didn't have two bedrooms I'd be sleeping on the couch. Well, it does have two bedrooms and I'm not sleeping anywhere but in *my* bed.'

'You deliberately misled me and you know it.'

'So sue me! Geez, A.J., I'm not slow on the uptake, you know... You aren't interested in re-creating the hot sex that got us into this situation in the first place—fine! I've got the message loud and clear.'

Amanda-Jayne felt herself blush, but wasn't sure if it was because he was so direct or so *close*. She pressed her hands against him to prise some distance between them, but the sensation of his firm, hard chest and beating heart beneath the fabric of his shirt filled her with an indecisive confusion that had her tilting her head back to look at him rather than breaking the bond of the arm around her waist.

As his dark eyes scanned her face, she felt as if all the air and everything else in the room had been vacuumed out and they were the only two physical objects remaining. She could hear nothing but the sound of her own pulse, feel nothing but the rhythm of his heart beneath her fingers. And smell nothing but the inciting scent of his maleness.

'I've never had to force myself on a woman and I'm not going to start now. And since you're pregnant and presumably not stupid enough to drink alcohol...'

'Of course not.'

'Then we shouldn't have a problem sharing a queen-size bed, should we?'

'*We won't?*' Her croaky voice drew his lips into a mouth-watering smile even as it snapped her from her sensual lethargy. 'And how exactly did you arrive at that conclusion?'

'Well, according to you, the only reason you were so *willing* to sleep with me before was because you were *drunk.* So, assuming you don't succumb to the evils of drink again, there should be no reason you shouldn't be as sexually averse to me as you are to Lethal. *Should there?*'

Alone the sexual challenge behind his words would have been sufficient impetus for her to shove free of him, but the mention of his dog at least gave her a less personal point of objection.

'Fine, we'll share the bed!' she snapped. 'But you keep that dog away from me.'

A wry smile lit his features. 'I guess I should be flattered that you prefer me to poor old Leth,' he muttered.

'That animal is a menace!' she told him, recalling the way he'd bailed her up against the wall as she'd tried to follow Reb up the stairs from the garage. 'I mean it, Reb; I don't want him anywhere near me.' She wished she could have kept the hint of panic from her voice, but she couldn't. She'd been utterly immobilised with fear by the dog's ferocious deep-throated growl until Reb had dropped her luggage and bounded back down the stairs to step between them. Though it had taken only one firm command from him to calm the dog and send him docilely on his way, Amanda-Jayne hadn't been that easily appeased.

While there was no way Reb could have known that as a teenager she'd seen her best friend savaged by a stray and been terrified of all but the smallest of dogs ever since, unlike others who'd witnessed her fear on similar occasions he hadn't laughed or accused her of being juvenile. Yet, in hindsight, even more surprising than his reaction to her was hers to him... She hadn't expected the strength of his arm closing around her to be quite so comforting, nor to have been so affected by his soothing words and the patience he'd displayed as he'd held her until her trembling subsided. Still, even just the thought of the huge hound unleashed downstairs made her uneasy.

'He won't hurt you, A.J.,' he reassured her, once more surprising her with his gentle tone. 'Savvy's had him since he was a puppy and I promise you his bark really is worse than his bite.'

'Yes, well, if it's all the same to you, I'd rather not have the experience of discovering that first-hand.'

'Okay, then, I'll tell Savvy he's not allowed to come upstairs again until you get used to him. Fair enough?'

With a curt nod she turned away from eye contact that made her feel too exposed, to survey the room.

This bedroom, like the apartment, was larger than she'd expected if much smaller than what she was used to. The wardrobe and chest of drawers adorned by a portable TV matched the bed's Federation style, but the two tartan arm-chairs situated at either side of the large window, while typical of the over-stuffed character of the forties and fif-ties, were clearly reproductions. On one wall hung a framed two-foot-by-four-foot photograph of a guy in red and black, racing leathers on a huge bike, leaning so far to one side his knee appeared to be skimming the ground; the photog-rapher must have snapped it a split second before the rider tipped the whole thing over.

With a colour theme of navy, dark green and white the room was as starkly masculine as Reb Browne, and Amanda-Jayne doubted she'd have been comfortable stay-ing in it even if she hadn't had to share it *and a bed* with him. Playing the optimist as best she could, she reminded herself that, with luck, the longest she'd have to endure this ordeal would be a week. Although she suspected a week of Reb's surly, in-your-face cousin Savannah would un-doubtedly equate to a lifetime. Honestly, the girl had all the social graces of a used teabag and less appeal!

What she *had* found appealing, however, was the horri-fied look on the face of Patricia's friend Eliza Montgomery when Amanda-Jayne had waved at her as she and Reb sped by the woman's house on their way here. No doubt about it, she thought with a smile, the local gossip mill would be working overtime by now... She'd give it three days tops before Patricia started phoning to beg and plead with her to 'come to her senses.'

And Amanda-Jayne *would* come to her senses, the instant her stepmother came good with the trust fund. Until then all she had to do was avoid Reb's obnoxious dog, keep out of the way of his even more obnoxious cousin and, since she clearly wasn't going to be able to avoid Reb himself, ignore the fact her traitorous hormones kept trying to conjure up memories of a night *that had never happened*!

'If you're up to it…' Reb's voice from behind startled her from her thoughts '…now would be a good time to come and meet the rest of the crew…'

'The crew?'

'Gunna and Debbie. Friends of mine who also work in the garage,' he explained. 'Oh, and you better put this on…' he said, tossing a small object towards her and startling her reflexes into action. 'I picked it up after I left your place last night.'

The guilt she felt on catching the small green leather jeweller's case was cloying. It only intensified when she opened it to see an emerald cut diamond set in white gold. *Oh, my!* Her mind gasped, before common sense reminded her that it could only be a cubic zirconia. A diamond this size would have been out of the price range of any motor mechanic, much less one who'd probably already blown his budget paying off her outstanding bills. Still, she knew no stone set in eighteen-carat white gold would come cheap because practically every item of jewellery she'd ever bought had to be specially made and had cost ten to twenty per cent more than an identical yellow or rose gold piece she could have bought off the shelf.

'It's…it's beautiful,' she said with utter truthfulness. 'But really, Reb, this wasn't necessary—'

'Yes, it was,' he cut in. 'There'll be a minority of people who are going to think we're getting married for exactly the reason we are—a one-night stand and a faulty condom. I don't want to invite that sort of public speculation. People who know me *know* I wouldn't shell out on a ring like that unless I'd lost both my heart and my mind,' he said dryly. 'And I'm damn sure none of your set would accept that you'd for settle some cheap and nasty engagement ring with a stone no one will notice.'

'Are you saying I'm a show-off?' she demanded.

He heaved a martyred sigh. 'No, that's *not* what I'm saying. But you can't deny you have expensive tastes and that—'

'*Excuse me!*' she objected. 'I have *good* taste, not expensive tastes.'

'Whatever. Just put the ring on. If it doesn't fit you can get it adjusted next time you go to Sydney to see your specialist.'

It fitted so perfectly that Amanda-Jayne felt a shiver go down her spine. Not only had he noted the fact that she didn't wear yellow gold, but he'd bought a ring in exactly her size. Cubic zirconia or not, she'd have to phone her insurance company and increase her cover. It was bad enough that Reb had spent so much money for the sake of an engagement ring she'd only be wearing for a week or so, but if anything happened to it in that time she'd feel even more awful.

'So, ready to head downstairs?' he said, interrupting her study of the ring glittering on her finger.

She nodded, then smiled. 'Reb, the ring really is beautiful. You've got good taste too.'

For a moment he stared at her with an intensity that had her legs starting to liquefy, then he spun on his heel and reefed open the door. 'No,' he grunted. 'Unfortunately I'm turning out to have expensive tastes.'

CHAPTER FIVE

IT OCCURRED to Reb that in the time since confronting Amanda-Jayne in Sydney he'd become complacent about the more obvious differences between her and the people he regarded as his friends, because they fair dinkum slapped him in the face when he introduced her to Debbie! The contrasts between the two women went far beyond the physical contrast of Amanda-Jayne's perfectly groomed elegance and Debbie's work uniform of cut-off shorts and a polo shirt emblazoned with 'BROWNE'S AUTO EMPORIUM.'

Though it was evident that Amanda-Jayne was uneasy about meeting his friends, she nevertheless pasted a smile on her face and was prepared to be pleasant and civil as good manners commanded; Debbie, however, barely raised her head from the invoices she was typing as they entered the garage office. Her patent lack of interest told him that not only had Savvy spread the word of Amanda-Jayne's unexpected arrival, but that his friend wasn't any happier with the current turn of events than she had been when he'd confirmed the rumours that he was responsible for Amanda-Jayne Vaughan's pregnancy.

'*What?*' she'd shrieked. 'I'd have thought you'd have more brains than to be suckered by some little rich chick out for a night on the wild side!' She'd been even more succinct when he'd adlibbed the fabrication that the relationship between him and A.J. was more than that.

Any expectations that she'd be more accepting of the situation on meeting Amanda-Jayne were blasted into oblivion within seconds of him completing the introductions, when Debbie barely stopped chewing her gum to grunt a bored, 'Hi,' before reverting her attention to her desk and grumbling, 'You better warn her not to dress like that every day, Reb. Around here grease isn't any more impressed by beige linen than it is denim.'

'It's raw silk, actually.' Amanda-Jayne's tone was patronising to the point of painful. 'But since I'm not the slightest bit impressed by grease I can assure you I'll be giving it and *anything* intimately acquainted with it a wide berth.'

Mercifully, before Debbie had a chance to verbalise the contempt which *that* remark had put into her eyes, the bearded, heavily tattooed Gunna suddenly stalked into the office. Smelling of petrol and wearing enough oil to do a dozen lube jobs, he cheerfully announced, 'Gidday, I'm Gunna,' as he thrust a large grimy hand towards a startled A.J.

Reb deemed it to A.J.'s credit that she hesitated for only a nanosecond before accepting his mate's hand into her own perfectly manicured one. 'Er, it's a pleasure to meet you, Gunther; I'm Amanda-Jayne Vaugh—'

'It's Gunna,' the burly ex-biker-cum-mechanic interrupted.

'Excuse me?'

'The name's Gunna…as in, gunna do this; gunna do that.'

The complete absence of any form of dawning comprehension on A.J.'s beautiful face had Reb torn between laughing and groaning. Unfortunately Debbie's reaction wasn't so indecisive and her raucous ridicule of Amanda-Jayne's perplexity immediately transformed his 'uptown fiancée's' expression into such regal indignation that Reb jumped into the firing line to prevent further verbal warfare.

'By the way, I wanted you guys to be the first to know Amanda-Jayne and I are getting married.' His words, however, didn't so much promote peace as all-encompassing cataleptic silence.

Gunna was in danger of standing on his jaw. Debbie looked as if she'd inhaled her ever present chewing gum.

And the woman who was supposedly wanting to marry him resembled someone sentenced to the electric chair.

Producing what he hoped was a convincing smile of pleasure, he dragged the obviously tense Amanda-Jayne to his side and gave her a warning squeeze. Taking the hint, she responded with a smile which captured the sort of self-conscious nervousness people probably expected from a newly engaged woman. Unfortunately, though, she didn't quit while she was ahead and the image was shattered when she said in her usual crisp, precise diction, 'We haven't formalised any arrangements yet. However, naturally I'm favouring something tastefully understated rather than the grand affair people around here are probably anticipating, since...' Her shoulders rose in a delicate shrug. 'Well, you understand... Suffice to say I'm not going to have the luxury of ten months to decide what dinner service pattern to use at the reception.'

Not surprisingly Gunna and Debbie's response to *that* was even slacker jaws and even more dumbfounded silence. Reb figured that Amanda-Jayne was doing her best, but he suspected that it was nervousness which had served to exaggerate her cultured upper-class tone and vocabulary to the point of making her seem even more bizarre to people whose experiences of wedding receptions were limited to the kegged beer and a backyard barbecue variety or a 'smorgasbord spread' catered by local women in the Scout hall. In a bid to ease the awkwardness of the moment he jokingly said that if choosing dinner china was that time-consuming they could all pretty well expect to be dining from nothing better than paper plates in four weeks' time.

As ice-breakers went, his humour had gone down like the *Titanic*.

'*You're marrying her in four weeks! Are you nuts?*' Debbie looked even more horrified than she sounded, but typically Gunna's response cut to the chase with even less tact.

'Geez, Reb! What's yer big hurry? Everyone already knows she's up the duff.'

Amanda-Jayne's face turned redder than her hair and Reb tightened his grip on her just in case rage, not embarrassment was the cause.

'Gunna, we aren't getting married just because she's pregnant,' he lied. 'We've been thinking about it for a while. Haven't we, sweetheart?'

At that point Amanda-Jayne looked even more surprised and bemused than his friends, but she must have studied drama at those posh schools she'd attended because before he knew what had hit him she'd kissed his cheek and given him the sexiest smile a man could imagine.

Damn, but that smile of hers had been hot enough to fry a man's guts! he reflected. Of course so was the you-are-dead-meat glare she was currently nailing him with as she lowered herself onto the extreme left-hand side of the mattress.

'If you so much as roll one millimetre onto my side of this bed,' she warned, her whisky eyes narrowing, 'your sex life is over for all time.'

'Now there's a comment that could be taken two ways…'

Amanda-Jayne wasn't in the mood to be teased. 'Yes. Seriously and *very* seriously.'

'How about *positively*?' he asked, his voice low. 'Because that statement *could* be interpreted as meaning that if I'm a good boy *on this occasion* I'll be rewarded on a future one…' He turned a lazy grin on her. 'Yeah, when you really analyse it, A.J., you have to concede those words hold more than a hint of sexual suggestion.'

'I won't concede any such thing! I assure you I was *not* trying to be one bit sexually suggestive!' she huffed, rolling over to turn her back to him.

'So what…? You always sleep in a seductive oversized T-shirt?'

'Of course not.'

'Then why do so tonight?'

'Because I've got nothing else t—'

'Aha! You like sleeping in the raw too, huh?'

'No, I— What do you mean, *too*?' she gasped, shock bringing her around to face him. 'Are you saying you're naked under that sheet?'

The grin he sent her was pure sin and so scrambled Amanda-Jayne's tired brain and jumbled emotions that it took her a second to register his hands lowering the sheet. Then several more seconds to silently admire the expanse of bare chest being revealed by the action… Bereft of a solitary molecule of fat, its contoured muscular tone had her fisting her hands in an attempt to nullify the burning desire of her fingers to explore each and every one of those perfectly contoured muscles. Could the light spattering of dark curls which narrowed the lower the sheet travelled really be as soft as she rememb—? *No!*

In less than a heartbeat she'd leapt from the mattress and put as much distance between her and the bed as was possible while her mind belatedly fought to override her errant libido. She remembered nothing of that night. *Nothing!*

'Hey, what's wrong?' Reb asked, his voice vibrating with amusement. 'Last time you saw these boxer shorts you laughed and said they were sexy.'

'Then that proves how drunk I was that night! Sober, I'd only ever consider a grown man wearing cartoon character underwear childish, not sexy,' she retorted, refusing to turn from the window in the hope the Southerly breeze would cool her overheated skin.

Why was she letting herself overreact to everything this man said and did when he obviously got some sort of perverse pleasure out of ruffling her feathers? Not that he'd been the only unsettling element she'd encountered in the eight or so hours she'd been here!

Never had she been in such an alien, not to mention *hostile* environment and been unable to rely on her social skills to come to her aid. It had been her intention before arriving to grit her teeth and smile through whatever trials she might encounter in the few days she'd have to spend here, but she'd not even made it up the stairs to the apartment before Hell's attack dog had eyed her as the chef's special.

Once inside the apartment surly Savvy had started snarling and bitten her head off for walking into her bedroom without knocking—something she'd never have done except that when Reb had indicated the two bedroom doors and said, 'That one is mine,' Amanda-Jayne, blissfully ignorant of Savvy's permanent resident status, had assumed the second was hers. Naturally, she'd apologised profusely, but because of the stupid agreement she'd made with Reb there wasn't any way she could excuse her apparently rude behaviour to his cousin's satisfaction and the girl, it seemed, held a grudge as a sponge did water.

'I was only teasing you, A.J....' Reb's voice reached from across the room to drag her mind back to the most recent of the stress-inducing moments she'd had today. 'Where's your sense of humour?'

'Obviously on a much higher level than yours.'

A masculine chuckle greeted her barb. 'Fair enough. But you can't stay up all night. Come back to bed. I won't lay a hand on you.'

'Oh, just go to sleep, will you? If I want to come to bed I will. If I don't I won't, okay?'

'Fine, fine. Suit yourself. No need to bite my head off.'

Yeah? Well, no one had a reason to bite mine off either, but everyone had a go at doing it today! she thought bitterly.

No sooner had she recovered from the antisocial attitudes of Reb's cousin and her oversized mutt than his employee friends had started in on her. Well, to be perfectly fair, the sinister-looking Gunna had proven relatively benign, but the gum-chewing Debbie had come out hissing and scratching without the slightest provocation. In fact such was her cattiness from the moment she'd laid eyes on her that Amanda-Jayne had assumed the pint-sized blonde with the guerilla-like personality must have been one of Reb's discarded lovers.

When she'd said as much to Reb he'd laughed fit to burst and explained that Debbie was in a long-standing, stable, de-facto relationship with Gunna which had produced one child, and the pair were making no secret of the fact they were actively trying to have another. The notion of the grizzly-sized ex-biker mating with the elfin, albeit razor-tongued Debbie seemed almost as incomprehensible as the circumstances of their relationship to Amanda-Jayne. Not because it was unheard of within her social circle for couples to live together out of wedlock, but to have children without the security of an airtight pre-nuptial agreement and marriage was regarded as financial and social suicide.

That thought prompted her to wonder if Reb mightn't be suspicious of the fact she'd not yet insisted on having a pre-nup drawn up. Her mistake in not pushing Anthony when he'd greeted her request for one with tearful accusations that she doubted his love had been rammed home when he'd run through her entire maternal inheritance just four years into their marriage. While she had no intention of marrying Reb, *he* didn't know that, so therefore he'd probably be expecting her to ensure the security of her future funds…

Gnawing her lip, she pondered the dilemma. At most it wouldn't take more than four days for the town gossip to get too much for Patricia to ignore. Four more days of being subjected to Reb Browne's warped sense of humour and the open animosity of his nearest and dearest wouldn't be easy, but she was confident she could handle it. Still…should she, for the sake of appearances, make a production of contacting her lawyers and having them draw up an agreement? On one hand it would be an utterly pointless exercise, but on the other it might just be the shove required to get Patricia into the game that much quicker.

Yes! She'd do it! The sooner Patricia was convinced her stepdaughter planned to marry Vaughan's Landing's resident bad boy, the sooner Amanda-Jayne could resume some semblance of her normal life. She expected Reb would be royally ticked off to discover that while he'd been smugly satisfied to hold all the aces she'd been biding her time with both the right and left bower and enough royalty in her hand to flat out euchre him! Not that she thought for a moment that he was the type of man to be a graceful loser in cards or anything else. No, undoubtedly he'd still insist on having some role in their child's life, but who knew? That didn't necessarily have to be a bad thing. After all, apart from being a tad bossy and taking obvious delight in provoking her, he seemed a basically decent guy—even if he did have a smile and a body that had her remembering things that bordered on indecent—like how his hands had—

Whoa! No, no, no!

She wasn't remembering anything! *Nothing.* Her mind was blank to last October the nineteenth. Completely and totally blank!

Taking a deep breath, she held it, willing her pulse to slow down. Repeating the action, she told herself she was exhausted, that was all. It had been a long, tiring couple of days both emotionally and physically; she needed to calm down and get a good night's sleep. She glanced at the bed and the sleeping form already occupying half of it, then, with a resigned sigh, slowly tiptoed towards it.

The nearer she got, the more impressive the view of Reb's smoothly muscular male back became; even in the darkness its deep even tan contrasted against the navy and white striped sheet. With effort she swallowed down a murmur of approval as hormonal excitement itched low in her belly.

'So he's got a great body,' she muttered angrily to herself. 'Get past it, Amanda-Jayne. *Sex is not going to solve your problems.*'

On that determined thought she slid beneath the sheets and willed herself to relax.

'Course, since you're already pregnant, sex isn't gonna add to your problems either.'

She ricocheted bolt upright. 'I thought you were asleep!'

He grinned. 'Not the first time you've made that mistake.'

'Maybe, but there's no way I'm going to repeat the one I made immediately prior to that! So would you kindly just give up, shut up and let me get some sleep?'

'Anything you say, A.J.' His soft laugh both tempted and taunted her. 'Sweet dreams.'

'Go to hell.' She pulled the pillow over her head, hugged it there for several seconds, then released it to add, 'And my name is *not* A.J.!'

'Reb!' The alarm in A.J.'s voice bothered him, but only until she appeared in the kitchen doorway still in the T-shirt she'd slept in, with her hair in sultry disarray. 'The bathroom door is locked!' she accused, her face tight.

Though he regarded himself as a morning person, in the wake of a night of erratic sleep and erotic dreams Reb wasn't in the right frame of mind to humour outraged females. Especially gorgeous, Titian-haired ones who were personally responsible for his restless night and the motivation behind the cold shower he'd recently endured.

'Gotta be up early if you wanna beat Savvy to the punch.'

She looked as if she might cry. 'Quick, then! Tell me where the other bathroom is!'

'Sorry, but you're slumming it now. We only have one. Downstairs—'

'You only have one bathr— Oh, no, I'm going to be sick!'

'Cut the theatrics, A.J.!' he snapped, spinning to face her then immediately lunging for the plastic trash bin by the patio door. He'd barely managed to complete the task before she snatched it from his grasp and held it to her face.

Gut-wrenching was definitely the only word to describe the next sound to fill the room and Reb cursed the helplessness that enabled him to do nothing more than keep a supportive arm around her and murmur inane reassurances.

He'd acknowledged that Amanda-Jayne Vaughan could rouse him on a sexual level, that she could irritate him through varying degrees of annoyance, anger and fury, but he hadn't counted on her being able to inspire his sympathy. Or that she could look quite so vulnerable and defenceless as she did now with her eyes awash with tears and her face chalk-white and damp with sweat, as she tried to regulate her breathing.

Her whispered request for a glass of water was such a relief that after guiding her to a chair he practically ran to the sink to fulfil it. The two tentative sips she took were no more reassuring to Reb than her croaked, 'Thank you. I'll be all right in a minute.' So, after disposing of the waste bin in the laundry, he scooped her up and, ignoring her feeble protests, carried her back to the bedroom.

It should have been easy for Amanda-Jayne to keep her eyes shut and let the gentleness of the hand caressing her cheek lull her to sleep, yet even in her less than sparkling current physical condition Reb Browne disturbed her on a far too elemental level for the action to promote inner tranquillity. Especially when her irresponsible hormones were still in a flap from the way he'd recently swept her into his arms and carried her to bed.

Refusing to speculate on how many other women had entered this room the same way, she promptly raised her eyelids, but not even knowing he was right there, sitting on the edge of the bed, prevented her heart from giving a silly little skip at the sight of his frowning, concerned face. Torn between thanking him for being so solicitous and telling him to go away so she could die without having to worry about how bedraggled she must look, she compromised with a grimaced smile.

'I've hustled Savannah out of the bathroom,' he said. 'So when you're up to it you can get dressed and I'll take you in to the doctor.'

'I don't need to see a doctor. It's only morning sickness.'

'Maybe it is,' he said. 'But it's also possible you've got a virus. All I know is that you haven't eaten anything except dry toast and tea since I picked you up yesterday and not even that has stayed down. My doctor wants me to bring you in as soon as you feel up to going.'

'Well, thanks all the same, but I'm not going. If I need to see a doctor I'll see my own, not some aged country quack.'

'I'll be sure and tell Carmel O'Brien that when we see her.'

Amanda-Jayne blinked. *You have a female doctor?*

'If I'm sick enough to warrant seeing a doctor, the last thing I worry about is their sex,' he said dryly. 'But Savvy reckons most women prefer female doctors so I figured you'd rather see Carmel.'

'Oh. Well, thank you for being so thoughtful,' she said, impressed that he had been. 'But like I said I don't need to see a doctor. So you might as well go and cancel the appointment.'

'A.J., you either go and see the doctor or I arrange for her to come here. I refuse to let you take chances with your health or the baby's. Now what's it to be?'

His flinty stare and stubbornly set jaw advised against suggesting anything else, but neither of those choices would gain her anything... *Or would they?*

'All right, I'll go!' she retorted, so as not to let him think she'd given in too easily. 'But in case you've forgotten you're a car doctor, not a people doctor. I'm only doing this to humour you, so don't delude yourself into thinking I'm going to jump to obey every time you issue an order, Reb Browne.'

'Oh, believe me, A.J., I'm sure I'll be institutionalised long before I ever get *that* delusional.'

They were welcomed into the doctor's surgery by the excited whispers and curious stares of the dozen or so people already seated in the waiting area. Every eye in the place was riveted to her and judging from the heat in her face Amanda-Jayne figured she'd blow the mercury out of a thermometer if one were to go in her mouth now. Silently she screamed at herself for not anticipating this.

The relief she felt when the receptionist rose from behind her desk and said the doctor had instructed her to be sent straight to an examination room was almost overwhelming. But it was as short-lived as the woman's very next words... 'This way, Reb, Ms Vaughan...'

For some reason both the smiling receptionist and Reb automatically assumed he would join them in the examination room and the proprietorial way he slipped his arm around her to guide her in the other woman's footsteps only further heightened the spectators' interest. Short of creating a scene for the dozen or so locals avidly watching them, Amanda-Jayne had no choice but to allow him to accompany her.

Expecting to have to wait while the doctor finished with her previous patient, it was a surprise to find her already in the examination room.

Though both Carmel O'Brien and her husband Ron had practised medicine in Vaughan's Landing for many years, they weren't the Vaughan family's practitioners and Amanda-Jayne knew them only by way of brief encounters at town social functions. On those occasions she'd found Carmel to be pleasant and likeable in a motherly, nononsense sort of way. On this occasion she was equally pleasant although Amanda-Jayne would have liked her a whole lot better had she not said that since there was a privacy screen Reb was welcome to stay in the room during the physical examination.

'I'm sure Amanda-Jayne will feel more comfortable knowing you're nearby,' she'd said.

Before Amanda-Jayne could deny that point, the doctor was taking her pulse and frowning. 'Your pulse is racing.'

Well, maybe if you shooed out the audience it wouldn't be! She had no time to verbalise the thought because a hand was suddenly clamped on her forehead.

'Don't even need a thermometer to tell your temperature is elevated. Who's your obstetrician?'

A tinge of panic started to knot her stomach and a quick glance at Reb told her he was bothered by the doctor's question too. 'Er…Dr Ralph Geermaine, in Sydney. Why? Is…is something wrong?'

Dr O'Brien smiled. 'Relax. It's my guess you've just got a viral infection, but for the sake of professional courtesy I'm going to call Dr Geermaine and let him know that you've come to see me and why. Since you're going to be living in my neck of the woods I'd also like to have a copy of your files.'

'My…my files?'

'Yes…if that's all right with you?'

'Well, er, sure. I…I guess so.'

'Do you happen to have his number on you?'

After hesitating a moment Amanda-Jayne nodded and opened her handbag.

Reb wondered why she was being so reticent. Frankly he was relieved that Carmel O'Brien wasn't going to just treat A.J. for the virus and leave it at that. He'd been bothered that her specialist was going to be so far away. Having Carmel close at hand and familiar with her medical history was a smart move.

'I hope you can get past his secretary,' A.J. said as she passed a business card to the doctor. 'I never can.'

The doctor smiled. 'In that case I'll be prepared to resort to the fact we were at med school together.'

This revelation only further reduced Reb's fears. 'So you

and this big city doctor were pals, were you, Carmel?' he teased. 'Where was Ron in those days?'

The older woman laughed. 'Knowing Ron he probably wasn't even aware there were any other male students in our class. I, however, was probably one of the few female students who *didn't* grovel at Ralph Geermaine's feet. There's no denying he's the best ob-gyn in the state these days, but back then I always thought he was a pompous jerk.'

Caught off guard by the doctor's candour, Amanda-Jayne only just stopped herself from saying, He still is! Privately, though, as much as she appreciated Carmel O'Brien's thoroughness in wanting to speak with her Sydney specialist, she felt dishonest putting the woman to so much trouble when this was going to be the one and only time she consulted her. Still, she could hardly admit that in Reb's presence.

'So aren't you going to apologise?' he asked forty minutes later as they walked to the local chemist for a herbal remedy Dr O'Brien had assured them was safe for pregnant women and would help minimise the symptoms of morning sickness.

'For what?'

'For doubting that a car doctor might know as much as a people doctor.' He laughed at her rolled-eyed response. 'I told you it was more than just morning sickness.'

'You just made a lucky guess in a two-horse race,' she said. 'And incidentally gloating is considered crass.'

'Oh, that worries me.'

She didn't give him the satisfaction of reacting to his sarcasm; she was more interested in spotting one of her stepmother's friends so she could make a point of introducing Reb to them and flashing the fake ring. It had been the opportunity to do that which had led her to give in to Reb's demands to come into town in the first place. Only problem was, this end of town wasn't exactly going to be thick with members of Patricia's bridge club.

'Reb, do you mind if we stop and have something to drink at the Fondue Café after we get this potion the doctor wants me to take?'

'Why go all the way up the other end of town? There's a milk bar right across from the pharmacy.'

She was saved from having to think of a good answer to that by the screech of brakes from a red Ferrari stopping in the middle of the street with no regard for the cars behind it.

'Geez,' she heard Reb mutter. 'Guess this is where I get to meet the rest of my future in-laws.'

Trying not to appear too elated at her unexpected stroke of luck, Amanda-Jayne gave a theatrically rueful shake of her head. 'Josh,' she said wearily. 'Are you deliberately trying to get your licence pulled or are you really a complete idiot?'

'Can I help it if Mum only bought me a second-hand car with cruddy brakes?'

'It's not the brakes that are cruddy, it's your driving.'

'Actually, A.J.,' Reb said, eyeing the car appreciatively, 'they did screech a bit too much considering he wasn't going that fast.'

Her brother's face positively beamed at the unexpected support. 'See, sis? And *he's* a mechanic. Hey, Browne,' he said, grinning. 'Do you give family discounts on brake work?'

Reb gave him an assessing look before glancing at the angry-looking driver in the car behind him. 'Maybe. But the guy behind you doesn't look real happy right now, so maybe you should pull over to the kerb and quit blocking traffic before you need a discount on dental work.'

The typical youthful arrogance with which Joshua Vaughan smiled and gave a cheeky wave to the horn-tooting driver behind him, before accelerating into a small kerbside space, both amused and irritated Reb. If one could get past the luxury car and what was obviously a three-figure haircut he had to concede the kid's behaviour and cockiness wasn't any worse than his own at the same age. Not that he and Joshua Vaughan would have anything else in common in their pasts. The future, however, was going to be a different proposition, he conceded, his gaze switching from brother to sister.

The family resemblance between them was limited to classic bone structure, well-bred good looks and dark eyes, the youth's blond hair and olive complexion being a stark contrast to A.J.'s straight copper locks and porcelain skin. But where only moments ago the woman beside him had looked almost deathly pale, her cheeks were now flushed with excitement and she could barely stand still as she went through the motions of introducing Josh to Reb. Then, with a beseeching and dazzling smile, she insisted they *simply must* cross to the milk bar for a chat.

In the absence of table service Reb offered to go and order for them, leaving Amanda-Jayne trying to read her brother's mind as his eyes followed the older man to the counter. But it wasn't what he might be thinking *now* that was important, but what impressions he went away with.

It was imperative that Josh believe that in mere weeks she really intended to enter the most unsuitable marriage of the century. Convincing him of this was crucial, because she didn't want Patricia to be left thinking that she'd back out at the last minute. But, not wanting to risk overkill, she decided to act casual and wait until her brother inevitably raised the subject of her impending marriage. It wouldn't, she knew, take him long.

'I wasn't expecting to bump into you,' she said casually. 'I thought you said you and a few friends were going to spend some time scuba-diving up in the Whitsunday Islands.'

'We are. But I'm not leaving until the day after tomorrow.'

'Oh. Well, I hope you have a nice time.'

'C'mon, sis,' he said wryly. 'My holiday plans are hardly

the most scintillating conversation we could having… So I'm going to be an uncle *and* a brother-in-law, huh?' He smirked, shaking his head slowly. 'Well, I'll have to congratulate you, Amanda-Jayne, if only because I didn't think you capable of pulling a stunt like this.'

'It's not a *stunt*, Josh.'

'Oh, right,' he said sceptically. 'Like you're genuinely in love with this guy.'

'I don't know why you find that so astonishing?'

He laughed. 'Let's just say I don't reckon even *love* could be that blind. Or stupid,' he said dryly. 'Of course I'd find it entirely believable if you said you were just doing this to get up Mum's nose. Not that I'd have credited you with being able to come up with anything this creative.'

Amanda-Jayne pasted an irritated expression onto her face. 'Josh, if you're going to be like this you might as well leave now. I won't have you saying anything to upset Reb.'

His expression turned to first disbelieving and then concerned. '*Upset* him? Sis, guys like Reb Browne don't get *upset*, they go ballistic and break beer bottles in people's faces.'

'Reb would *never* do anything like that,' she said instinctively, before adding with a soft artful intensity, 'He wouldn't, Josh. Besides, do you really think I'd marry someone like that?'

'You tell me. According to rumours the happy event is only four weeks away. Mum is going to be apoplectic when she hears.'

'*When* she hears? You mean she doesn't know?'

Josh shook his head. 'Not yet. But only because she's been staying at Aunt Rachel's in Melbourne since the run-in the two of you had at New Year's. She's due back tomorrow and I can guarantee she'll be frothing at the mouth when she finds out.'

Josh must have interpreted Amanda-Jayne's relieved sigh as one of despair for he smiled ruefully and said, 'C'mon, sis, you can't honestly have believed she was egalitarian enough to quietly accept you shacking up with a local criminal?'

Amanda-Jayne tightened both her face and voice. 'I'm not *shacking up* with him, Josh. I'm planning to marry him as soon as legally possible.'

'Oh, yeah, well, that'll make her feel better…*not*.'

'How Patricia feels about things isn't the issue here, Josh. It's *my* feelings that count. And Reb's, of course,' she tacked on, hoping to sound suitably loving. 'Besides, it's not as if your mother and I have ever shared a close relationship. We're not exactly the Brady Bunch.'

Her brother's face tightened uncomfortably and he momentarily averted his gaze. 'Look, I know I've always been Mum's favourite, but that's not my fault.'

Surprisingly the admission made Amanda-Jayne feel closer to her brother than she had for many years and for a second she stepped away from the charade she was playing.

'I know that, Josh,' she said gently. 'I don't have anything against you. Your mother and I were at odds long before you were born. Which,' she said, pulling herself up before she got sentimental, 'is precisely why she's got no reason to expect me to bow to her wishes, call off the wedding and walk away from the father of my child.'

'She'll expect it because, as we've been told from the cradle, the Vaughans have an image to uphold and you're a Vaughan.'

'Not for much longer.' She produced a suitably dreamy smile that brought a deep frown to Josh's eighteen-year-old face.

'You're actually saying you're *really* in love with this guy?'

Again she was creatively evasive. 'Considering what Anthony put me through, do you think I'd entertain marriage again for any other reason?'

Her brother stared at her for a moment, before despairingly shaking his head and slumping back in his chair.

'Then you better be prepared for Mum to use every trick in the book to stop you.'

'Oh, don't worry, Josh…' She smiled. 'I'm prepared for that.' *Matter of fact I'm counting on it!*

CHAPTER SIX

REB had always thought her beautiful but now, as she looked from him to her brother with an uncertain smile and wide, bemused eyes—as if she wasn't sure if she was dreaming or not—she was breathtaking…ethereal almost. He'd had the impression she and Josh weren't particularly close, but her brother's unexpected appearance today proved otherwise. Reb's previous estimation of the kid rose considerably; it took a fair bit of strength of character to escort your sister down the aisle when your own mother had fled the country rather than endure the social backlash of her marriage. Nor surprisingly Reb's opinion of the absent Patricia Vaughan hadn't changed one iota; she was a bitch of the first order.

For all A.J.'s claims of the past few weeks that she was fine now her morning sickness was gone, Reb knew she'd been battling to deal with acute bridal jitters and her inability to reconcile or even contact her stepmother. Unable to locate her vacationing brother to find out Patricia's whereabouts, all of A.J.'s other enquiries had effectively been stonewalled by the woman's friends, relatives and even the family solicitors. Oh, yeah, Patricia Vaughan had gone to great lengths to ensure her stepdaughter knew precisely how she felt about her marrying the town's bad boy. Reb personally didn't give a damn what the woman thought of him, but he'd been furious that her behaviour was creating unnecessary stress for his pregnant bride-to-be and as a consequence making *his* life crazy.

In the last week A.J.'s moods had swung between raging tempers and hours of withdrawn silence and Reb hadn't managed to successfully anticipate one of them. At any time of the day or night she'd disappear in that car of hers for long solo drives to who knew where, leaving Reb worried sick until he again heard her swinging into the garage. His concern was such that he'd actually spoken to Dr O'Brien. The doctor had reassured him that most of A.J.'s behaviour was due solely to the hormonal stress, but also conceded that it wasn't unreasonable to assume that despite the past fraught relationship with her stepmother she might have secretly hoped that her pregnancy and upcoming marriage would rectify the problems. Accepting that wasn't going to happen would naturally be difficult for her.

Reb tried to find some solace in the doctor's words, but it wasn't easy. Hell, it was next door to impossible! A.J. reacted to even his most innocent remark or suggestion with either screams or tears and managed to get both herself and him so strung out that he'd not only worried about whether *they* could hold things together until the baby arrived, but whether Savvy and the garage staff would emerge psychologically unscathed.

Maybe this marriage was all just a charade, but he'd be eternally grateful that Josh had appeared from nowhere in time to walk his sister down the aisle, because Lord knew how she'd have managed it solo, such was the way her hand was trembling as Josh passed it into Reb's. Maybe once this stupid ceremony was out of the way they could settle into some semblance of a normal life.

Amanda-Jayne was convinced she was going to faint. No, she *prayed* she would—if only to forestall the inevitable a few moments longer. *It was never supposed to come to this.* This wasn't how her well thought out plan was to have panned out. She looked up into the handsome face of the man standing beside her and felt her heart give a hysterical lurch. It gave another as his mouth stretched into a gentle smile and he gave her hand a reassuring squeeze.

Oh, God, help me out here! she beseeched in silent hysteria. *Flood, earthquake, instant death—anything will do!*

The minister cleared his throat to attract their attention. 'Are you ready to commence?'

Amanda-Jayne's denial stuck in her throat. Her mental scream of no was ignored by everyone, even as her knocking knees had to be registering on the Richter scale. Panic washed through her body in tumultuous waves as her brain urged her to run and instinct demanded she stay. Or was it the other way around? Her instincts telling her to bolt for the exit as fast as her jelly-like legs would carry her and her brain reasoning that to do so would only further damage her farcical life?

'Amanda-Jayne?' the minister murmured impatiently. 'Are you ready to begin the ceremony?'

How ironic *he* should be hurrying her now. After Reb had booked him to perform the service, he'd telephoned Amanda-Jayne urging her not to overreact to her 'unfortunate lapse into promiscuity' by rushing into an ill-conceived marriage. At the time she'd doubted he'd noticed his pun, but she'd had no doubts that his pastoral concern came at the direction of her stepmother, camouflaged behind a further donation towards restoration of the church's pipe organ.

Under the judgmental stare of the minister the leaden silence in the church seemed to rise to a crescendo that kept rhythm with her galloping heart and frenzied thoughts. She tightened her grip on Reb's hand in the hope of absorbing the abundance of confidence he always radiated and tried to calm her thoughts. If anything the reassuring pressure his fingers delivered to hers only caused her more internal chaos. Why was it her only support was coming from a direction she didn't want to go in?

In the end she decided it wasn't only *her* future which was at stake, but that of her unborn child. And in the absence of Patricia riding up the aisle on a white charger waving a cheque her only option was to go with the flow. Taking a deep breath, she nodded to the minister...

* * *

'Harley Rebel Browne, do you take—?'

The minister's words snapped Amanda-Jayne from the daze she'd retreated into in the hope of surviving the ceremony. *Harley Rebel?* Her gaze flew to Reb's face, but the tight line of his mouth and the faint tinge of pink beneath his tan confirmed her ears *were* working properly. Oh, dear Lord, she was marrying a man who'd been named after a motorcycle! If this was a hard and fast tradition in the Browne family he'd probably want to call their child Kawasaki or Ducati or who knew what.

Well, she wouldn't have it! She wouldn't! Call her conservative, but she'd call her baby Moonbeam or Litmus Paper before she let it be named after a brand of motorbike! For the remainder of the service Amanda-Jayne's responses worked on auto-pilot, while her mind frantically catalogued a list of alternative names for their child.

'Harley and Amanda-Jayne, I now pronounce you husband and wife. Harley, you may kiss your bride.'

As his mind echoed the minister's words Reb told himself that kissing her was just part and parcel of the ceremony, *not* the opportunity to release the brain-numbing desire he'd been forced to shackle each night lying beside her warm, tempting body. God and half of the population of Vaughan's Landing were watching them at this moment and he wasn't about to seize either it or her like some lust-crazed fool. At least he wasn't until his hands closed over her bare shoulders and the flare of desire lighting those whisky-brown eyes as they lifted to his caused a sensation almost identical to the one he'd got as a kid when he'd mixed up the battery terminals on a mate's car.

He would have liked to credit his reaction to pure lust, but he couldn't entirely buy the story. In that nanosecond of time the full ramifications of the vows they'd just exchanged dawned. 'For richer for poorer, in sickness and in health, in good times and bad...'

Reb figured the last four weeks had pretty much proved he could handle the sickness and health part; the good times and bad…well, surely things could only get better on that score? But the richer and poorer part filled him with a whole heap of dread… Three years from now Amanda-Jayne Vaughan was again going to be too rich to need him. He'd known that going in, of course. The problem was, until now the notion hadn't bothered him. *Now*, however, the thought of losing her had his chest cavity feeling as if it was full of lead. He had the horrible feeling that fate had just kicked him in the backside.

Amanda-Jayne felt herself blush as Reb's obvious reluctance to kiss her started to draw cat calls and encouragement from people sitting on his side of the church. Never before had her pride been so publicly trampled and it was only etiquette which stopped her saying, Hey, listen, I'm not exactly salivating at the thought of kissing you either, buster! Well, etiquette and the fact that if he continued to caress her shoulders like that she'd prove herself a liar in no time flat; the lazy heat he was inducing in her body was making her dizzy in ways that had nothing to do with her condition.

In a bid to take control of both her renegade hormones and a situation fast becoming so farcical it would probably end up in town folklore, she pasted a smile on her face and stepped forward to place her hands on his chest. Her action provoked not only cheering but several whistles and had the minister clearing his throat and reminding the rambunctious congregation where they were.

Ignoring the cluster of hyperactive butterflies in her belly, she rose on her toes until her face was only inches from his, to bravely whisper, 'Look, I think you better kiss me. Your friends are on the verge of rioting.'

In an instant her urgent, husky suggestion had totally banished Reb's good intentions to keep a safe distance between them and limit himself to just a chaste brush of her lips. His fingers ploughed into her hair and in less than a heartbeat he parted her lush mouth beneath his.

So this is what water tastes like to a parched man in the

desert! Until the thought registered in him, Reb hadn't known the full extent of his need to again possess Amanda-Jayne's mouth. He'd told himself that abstinence had merely sharpened his sexual desire and that his imagination had embroidered the passion she'd aroused in him that night in Sydney. But abstinence and imagination couldn't be held responsible for the glorious relief he felt flowing through him from something as simple as a wedding kiss.

Simple? Ha! There was nothing simple about any of this. This beautiful, sexy, sophisticated woman was now his wife. A concept which seemed as bizarre as it did incredibly right. On every conceivable level their tastes were poles apart, but Reb knew he'd never be satisfied with the taste of any other woman now that his tongue was reacquainted with the unique flavour of Amanda-Jayne Vaughan.

Moving his hands to the smooth softness of her face so he could better savour the soul-destroying sweetness of her mouth, he was once more almost paralysed by the sheer beauty of his mental image of her rounded with his child. How many nights had he leapt from the bed and sought sanctuary in the garage, afraid he'd succumb to the almost overwhelming desire to slip his hand beneath her nightwear and flatten his palm against her still visually flat belly? And now... Dear Lord, now she was returning his kiss with an ardour to match his own and pressing it against him...

At the first touch of his lips against hers Amanda-Jayne gave herself up to the kiss, the sounds of the congregation drowned out by that of her own pulse and the echoes of a night almost four months previous. She knew then she'd been naive in telling herself she'd blocked out all the memory of this man's kisses, for every nuance of his taste and touch was as familiar and unforgettable to her as if they'd been tattooed on her instincts, her mind and her soul; as if she'd kissed him a million times in a million past lives. Perhaps they had been lovers in a past life, for there was no other way she could rationalise, justify or even explain the sense of oneness she felt in Reb's arms.

When he deepened the kiss he bombarded her with so many conflicting emotions, on both a sensual and spiritual level, she felt both safe and at risk—as if she was simultaneously floating and plummeting from a great height. In a bid to anchor herself, or at least slow her free-fall, she flung her arms around his neck and held on for all she was worth. Yet it was futile to think the solid masculine strength of his body could stabilise her either mentally or physically for the tighter she held him, the more scrambled her brain became and the weaker her knees got. Strangely, though, on another level she felt saner and stronger than she had at any other time in her life. With every stroke of his tongue against hers, every movement of his hands against her body, she was aware of not just her courage and her hope spiralling, but of a growing sense of joy.

The sound of a satisfied masculine moan deep in Reb's throat drew a matching one from her and sent a shower of pleasure racing down her spine. Her pulse was pounding at lightning speed, the butterflies previously wreaking havoc in her stomach invaded her veins and arteries and it was obvious her hormones didn't know how to behave in church— *Oh, Lord! They were in a church!*

The first thing to register with Reb after A.J. abruptly pulled away was that her face was beetroot-red. So was the minister's. Except whereas A.J. merely looked embarrassed the man of the cloth looked almost apoplectic. Reb told himself it was his rowdy friends behind him who'd spun the man out; after all, the good vicar had been the one who suggested the kiss, so there was no reason why he should be looking daggers at Reb. Unless, of course, the guy was a mind-reader…

The inane thought was almost enough to make Reb feel guilty. Almost. It didn't stop him from grinning as the organist started up and an embarrassed A.J. slipped her arm through his for the journey out of the church.

'Till death do us part, huh?' Reb said softly. 'Guess that means that if you ever look more beautiful than you do today I'll be around to see it.'

The sentiment and the implication of his words brushed against her heart, causing it to stagger so much she was momentarily physically unbalanced. Instantly Reb's hand was on her elbow. Her eyes flew to his, trying to gauge his sincerity. Did he really think she was beautiful? More importantly, did he mean to imply that he was prepared to make their marriage work…to last until death parted them? Or was he simply upping the ante to get her into his bed?

You're already in his bed, you goose! her brain chided. *What you really want to know is if he's planning on pushing the issue of sex.*

I'm not! her morals argued.

Ha! Like he'd have to push, her hormones injected wryly, causing her to remember how she'd responded to his kiss. At that moment she caught Josh's eye and his cheeky wink had her inwardly cringing at the public spectacle she'd just made of herself. By this time tomorrow the creativity of local gossip would have her having dragged Reb onto the floor and ravishing him. She stifled a groan as one of her chatty inner voices pointed out that such a scenario had probably only been avoided by about thirty seconds.

Because she'd never posted ninety-five per cent of the invitations she'd made such a production of writing, only a handful of her friends were likely to have witnessed the blatant display of passion she'd just put on, but she didn't doubt for one minute they'd eagerly relate this entire event. It was bad enough that the church had been packed with friends of Reb's and curious locals who'd be gossiping about her for years to come, but by tomorrow she'd be the talk of Sydney's social set as well. She sighed. It was time to face facts; her once pristine reputation was definitely hurtling towards the first stages of rigor mortis.

Unable to bring herself to turn and smile at the people crowding both sides of the church as Reb did, she kept her gaze fixed firmly on the double doors which seemed a hundred miles away. As she'd done coming into the church she concentrated on putting one foot steadily in front of the other, but unlike her entrance she wasn't trembling nor on the verge of tears; now she just felt kind of disoriented, as if she was in a daze. Or perhaps in a state of shock was a more accurate description—Lord knew her reaction to Reb's kiss had been shocking—but so too was the reality that she'd been caught in a trap of her own inept making.

As of now she was living proof of the adage that cheats never prosper. She'd been manipulative, calculating and deliberately devious and in all fairness she had to concede that Reb deserved better. In the past four weeks he'd not only tried to ease her lifestyle transition, but he'd honoured every promise he'd made when they'd entered into their engagement—whereas she'd never had any intention of marrying him and had made no real effort to get on with him, his cousin, his friends, or to fit into life at the garage.

She would have liked to be able to vow that she'd turn over a new leaf starting now, but the truth was she wasn't any more certain that she could cope with the direction her life had taken than she had been four weeks ago. All she could do was promise herself she would *try* to be a good wife to Reb. For the next three years she'd honour both her vows and the arrangement they'd entered into four fateful weeks ago.

Watching the black Saab speed out of a car park crammed with beat-up trucks and motorbikes, Amanda-Jayne couldn't decide if it had been the drunk, overly amorous biker or the idea of eating home-made tuna casserole in a Scout hall decorated with crêpe paper streamers which had prompted her old school chum Roberta Winchester-Barry to depart so early; although she was honest enough to acknowledge that even as recently as yesterday either one would have been enough to send her screaming into the streets too. It hurt that the woman she'd always considered her closest friend hadn't stuck out the reception, but it infuriated her that Robbie had felt it necessary to comment that she hoped Reb was as good in the sack as he looked as if he'd be, because she couldn't find one other reason for Amanda-Jayne marrying the likes of him otherwise—pregnant or not!

'If anyone takes a photo of you now they could title it *The Homicidal Bride*.'

'Josh!' She spun around and faced not only her brother but her recently acquired husband.

'Gee, sis, you seem almost as surprised to see me now as you did at the church this morning.'

'Not quite,' she said dryly. 'That was the surprise of the century.'

'Surely you didn't think I'd miss my only sibling's wedding?' he teased.

'Considering your mother hasn't even bothered to call,' Reb said, 'I'm glad someone in A.J.'s family made the effort.' He slipped an arm around her waist and drew her against his side; the casual action sent a shower of tingles down her spine and low into her abdomen. The sensation was only marginally less disruptive to her pulse than the one he'd set off as he'd glided her around the floor in a very proper but sensually disorientating Bridal Waltz. Amanda-Jayne had found herself torn between relief and disappointment when, immediately the dance ended, he'd guided her back to the bridal table and then disappeared.

Now he was back, holding her close to his side, and once again her brain and libido were bickering over how much she should read into his actions; it took enormous concentration to try and stay focused on what her brother was saying.

'So what sort of family discount do I get on all my mechanical work?' he was asking Reb.

'All your mechanical work?' Reb raised an eyebrow. 'I thought you were only after a brake job.'

Josh grinned. 'Nah, my efforts as matchmaker are worth much more than that.'

'How,' Reb asked, 'do you figure that?'

'Well, gee, Reb, if I hadn't managed to convince Mum that trying to talk Amanda-Jayne out of marrying you was a lost cause she'd have probably turned up today and dragged her out of the church.'

Reb laughed.

Amanda-Jayne didn't. 'Y-y-you talked Patricia out of—'

'Yep!' Josh proudly overrode her stammering. 'Told her that if she wanted to save herself a whole heap of anguish she should make herself scarce until she got used to the idea of Reb as a son-in-law, because I'd spoken to you and you were dead set on getting married.

'Hey, don't look so stunned, sis,' he said. 'I know you've had a rough few years, what with all your health problems, then Dad dying and your jerk of an ex...' He shrugged self-consciously. 'I know that's all behind you now but I just decided it was about time someone in the family was in your corner.'

Panic gripped Reb as A.J. suddenly went limp against him and only the instinctive tightening of his arm prevented her from fainting onto the ground.

CHAPTER SEVEN

'OH, MY God!'

Savvy's horrified scream bounced off every wall and almost sent Amanda-Jayne through the ceiling.

'Reb!' the teenager urged at the top of her voice. 'Reb, hurry! I think she's trying to kill herself!'

It hadn't occurred to Amanda-Jayne before that the girl might have a drug problem; it did now. Either that or she was certifiable and Amanda-Jayne was determined not to look away from her. She told herself to stay calm, that Reb would know how to handle this. Reb would be able to—
Oh, my!

Amanda-Jayne's thoughts skidded to a halt as his sudden appearance sent her mind cart-wheeling out of control, clogged her lungs and placed calm way outside her immediate reach! It was one thing to steel herself to hug the edge of the mattress with her back turned to him and her eyes squeezed tightly shut when he climbed into bed each night, but there wasn't a woman alive who could have blinked, much less ignored the sight Reb Browne presented now. He was quite simply walking sexuality.

Except he wasn't walking. He was standing...barefoot, bare-chested and securing a towel around his hips.

Savvy's blood-curdling scream had obviously interrupted his shower. Or perhaps, given the traces of shaving foam hugging his rugged masculine face, he'd been shaving. Either way he was the most provocative sight Amanda-Jayne had ever seen before breakfast, but as those soul-stirring black-brown eyes fixed on her, flashing seven types of fire, the hunger he stirred in her had nothing to do with omelettes.

Dry-mouthed, she could only shake her head when he demanded, 'What is going on here?'

'Isn't it obvious?' his cousin responded. '*She's got a carving knife.* And you might as well know right now, if she's going to off herself in the kitchen, *I'm* not cleaning up the blood.'

'*What?*' Amanda-Jayne exclaimed, the absurdity of the girl's statement reefing her from her salacious stupor. 'Oh, for—' She threw the innocent but incriminating knife into the sink. 'I'm *preparing breakfast.*'

The teenager reeled back against the wall and, arms splayed, sent a desperate look to Reb. 'It's worse than I thought. *She's planning to kill us.*'

'Then she'll have to form a line behind me to get to you!' Reb snapped at her. 'I don't appreciate your warped sense of humour this early in the morning.'

'I don't reckon anything she cooks will be too appealing to you either. It's not like she's spent any time in the kitchen since she's been here,' Savvy sneered. 'Do you honestly think a week of marriage automatically gives her cooking skills?'

'*Savannah…*' Reb's tone was all the more menacing for its low pitch. '*That's enough.* Now, I suggest that if you haven't fed Lethal yet you go and do it, otherwise you can go to your room until it's time for breakfast.'

'Yes, sir, no, sir, three bags full, sir!'

'Don't push me, Savvy,' he warned.

An insolent smirk edged its way across the teenager's pretty but bizarrely made up face. Despite the fact Amanda-Jayne was convinced she applied her eyeliner with a paint roller, she couldn't fail but be impressed at the way she stubbornly stood her ground under Reb's direct glare. She doubted few men would have been game enough to challenge such visual hostility and Lord knew most females wouldn't have been immune to such a concentrated exposure of raw sex appeal. *Her* pulse rate still hadn't stabilised.

'I'm not kidding, Savannah,' Reb said dangerously

softly. 'Believe me, I'm not in the mood to wear your cheek on top of…everything else.'

'Everything else being Miss-I'm-too-good-to-breathe!' his cousin flashed, then, as if only now recognising Reb's ever tightening jaw, quickly added, 'Oh, all right! All right! I'll go feed Leth.' With a final narrow-eyed glance at Amanda-Jayne she crossed to the door of the stairwell and reefed it open.

If the number of times her feet stamped following her departure was any indication, Amanda-Jayne figured she was halfway down the steps before she 'bravely' shouted, 'Say, Reb! Don't expect me to eat anything she tries to cook—*you* married her; let *your* stomach suffer the consequences!'

Reb muttered a curse, then heaved a sigh that did wonderful things to his chest and played havoc on Amanda-Jayne's nervous system. He caused her more internal damage by moving to gently grasp her shoulders as his brown-black eyes slowly studied her face.

'You okay?' he asked.

Barely; but you move an inch closer and it's short odds I'll melt at your feet.

No sooner had her mind registered the thought than he *did* move closer and the realisation that she must have spoken aloud and that he was picking up the challenge brought a pained groan from her throat. His gaze darted to her mouth, causing a million butterflies to begin fluttering in her stomach; he was going to kiss her. Again… For eight days and nights she'd replayed their wedding kiss over and over. Now she was going to have a chance to *relive* it. Only this time they wouldn't be in a church and there'd be no disapproving minister nor rowdy spectators to keep her emotions in check. That thought alone caused her breath to catch and her body to sway. She closed her eyes as the heat of his hands tightening on her forearms began to seep through her, creating a blend of fearful excitement and dizzying expectation until she was literally shaking with it…

Alarmed by her long, distracted silence and the tension her body was transferring to his hands, Reb gently shook her.

'*A.J.?*' he said urgently. 'A.J., answer me… Are you all right?'

Those seductive whisky eyes flew open then blinked twice before her face flamed and her palms pushed viciously at his chest. The contact paralysed him momentarily, before his most basic instincts prompted him to grasp her wrists to prevent her withdrawal.

'Let me go! For heaven's sake, I'm not suicidal!'

He automatically tightened his hold as he searched her face for a clue to her sudden hostility.

'What?' She glared at him. 'You honestly believe I was going to stab myself to death?'

'Don't be stupid. What's wrong?'

'Your cousin's sick sense of humour scared ten years off my life, that's what!' she snapped. 'One minute I'm alone with my thoughts of Spanish omelettes; the next she creeps into the room and starts carrying on like some sort of drug-crazed banshee!

'Earlier she barged into the bathroom while I was brushing my teeth and jumped into the shower ahead of me!' she went on hotly. 'She acts like she owns this place.'

'She does. Well, fifty per cent of it anyway,' Reb said, before checking his tongue. Not wanting to get into a discussion which might lead to questions about his financial status, he seized on her other comment. 'Regardless of how difficult Savvy can be at times, I can assure you she isn't stupid enough to mess with drugs. Believe me, with my background I'd recognise a problem like that in a second.'

'Really? Well, have you noticed that your…*difficult* cousin hates my guts? That she goes out of her way to either insult or ignore me?'

'I've noticed. But she's only fifteen and I can't say I've seen you making too much effort to befriend her either.'

Perfectly arched eyebrows shot up indignantly. '*Excuse*

me? I've not said one angry word to Savvy since I moved in.'

'Nor one friendly one either, I'll bet.'

'That's because she starts snarling and throwing me dirty looks the moment she sees me.'

'That's not how it looks from where I've been standing, A.J.'

'Then either you're standing in the wrong spot or your eyes need testing!' she retorted. 'Ever since the wedding I've gone out of my way to avoid confrontations with Savannah, and—'

'And before that you went out of your way to avoid *everyone*, including me,' he cut in sagely. 'Everyone's been willing to make allowances for you because you've had an unfamiliar lifestyle thrust on you and you're pregnant, but it's time you started meeting them halfway.'

Amanda-Jayne could only stare at him. *No one* had made *any* allowances for her. He was being totally unfair. Some of her dismay must have shown on her face for his expression suddenly became rueful and he gave an exasperated sigh.

'Okay, that didn't come out completely right. What I'm trying to say is when Savannah starts needling you, instead of responding with that condescending, snooty down-your-nose stare of yours and expecting me to intervene on your behalf, you should stand up to her. Give her back some of her own. You'll earn her respect a lot quicker that way.'

Amanda-Jayne mentally counted to ten. But only to ensure her anger wouldn't transpose anything of what she intended saying to the semi-nude, condescending man standing in front of her.

'So,' she said with deceptive calm. 'What you're saying is that the next time Savvy does something like this and starts bellowing like a wounded bull—for no reason—instead of instinctively standing rigid with astonishment, I should rush her, flatten her against the wall and tell her that if she doesn't shut up I'll strangle her?'

An amused smile broke over the poor, unsuspecting fool's face. 'Maybe nothing *that* confrontational, but a firmly delivered "Pull your head in" will usually snap her back into line.'

'And does it work as effectively with you?' she asked casually.

He frowned. 'With me?'

His innocent tone snapped her thinly reigned temper. 'Yes, with you! You arrogant, patronising...*brute*!' she roared, shoving him hard enough to make him stagger and allowing her to advance from the sink. 'Don't you dare criticise and lecture to me about not making an effort to fit in around here. I'm trying, damn it! For the last week I've gone out of my way to be friendly to Gunna and Debbie and all either of them do is *grunt* at me.

'Now, since Gunna smiles when he grunts,' she went on, 'I assume that he's being friendly, but Debbie's just plain rude. I mean, even that ugly mutt Lethal has started wagging his tail while he's growling at me, but not Debbie. Oh, no! She makes snide comments or mutters under her breath at every opportunity.

'Well, get this—' she jabbed a finger at him '—I'm sick of it! I'm sick of being on the receiving end of some sort of inverted snobbery and treated with ridicule! I'm sick of being treated like this whole situation is *my fault*. *You* were the one who insisted on this marriage, Reb, and I'm sick to death of having your family and your friends punishing me for agreeing to it. Furthermore—'

'Okay, okay,' he cut in, holding his hands palms upward. 'Don't get your knickers in a knot. Just settle down and—'

'I'm not wearing knickers! And what's more I *won't* settle down! I'll admit I mightn't have been easy to live with before we got married, but I've bent over backwards since then to try to achieve harmony in this place.

'I haven't complained about how your cousin waits until I'm on my way to the bathroom before rushing in head of me, slamming the door in my face and then staying in there longer than it takes to perform a heart-lung transplant. I've bitten my tongue at her sarcasm and meekly continued passing on all her stupid phone messages even though her friends take great pleasure in facetiously calling me ''Ma'am'' and ''Mrs Browne''.

'And now this morning,' she said, 'when I especially get up early with the sole intention of cooking everyone a delicious breakfast, she starts World War Three and it's *my* fault!'

Amanda-Jayne knew she was shouting, but she was surprised to find tears sneaking down her cheeks. Refusing to have her anger mistaken for hysteria, she roughly wiped them away.

'A.J.... Hon—'

'I'm not finished!' She evaded the placating hand Reb extended. 'As far as I'm concerned, Reb Browne,' she continued, 'we might not be sleeping together in the accepted sense of the word, but we *are* married and I'm carrying your child; I think that entitles me to some modicum of emotional spousal support and loyalty. So I'd appreciate it if you weren't so quick to jump down my throat and blame me for every drama that crops up in future.'

She took a long, steadying breath and waited expectantly for him to say something, but no immediate comment was forthcoming. His handsome face remained unreadable as his dark eyes slowly swept over her. As always he managed to make her feel painfully self-aware and not a little foolish, but she fought down the instinct to bolt from the room; if she was prepared to make sacrifices to get through the next three years of this marriage everybody else had better expect to do likewise! She might have a bit of paper stating she was a Browne by marriage, but unfortunately she was a Vaughan by birth and upbringing, and if ever there were two roles she was inherently ill-equipped to assume they were those of whipping boy and silent suffering martyr!

As she stood there, gloriously challenging, with her hands clamped on her hips, her eyes bright with expectation and her chin tilted in unmistakable defiance, Reb found himself amused, awed *and getting more aroused with every passing second*. A fact his towel wasn't going to be able to keep a secret for too much longer. It had been difficult enough to keep his attraction to her in check from the first night they'd shared a bed. In the days since her passionate response to his kiss on their wedding day, his libido had come close to turning him into a nervous wreck. While he was certain a session of hot and heavy sex would go a long way to restoring his equilibrium, after weighing up the pros and cons he'd decided that it was best to wait until she was better adjusted to their current situation before commencing a concentrated seduction campaign.

But that was before she'd stood in front of him, lit by the morning sun, with her silky copper hair falling over her shoulders, a thigh-high T-shirt exposing the best pair of legs he'd ever seen, and boldly announced she was naked beneath it. For all his good intentions, considering his own minimalist attire, this moment couldn't be interpreted as anything but opportunity knocking and he didn't have the strength to walk away from it. If he was wrong, then Amanda-Jayne would undoubtedly use all her weight to slam the hypothetical door on his fingers, but the memory of how that weight had felt lying along his sweat-slicked body four months ago made the risk seem worthwhile.

She was the most beautiful, sexy woman he'd ever known…and he ached to know her again. Every glorious, soft millimetre of her—her firm high breasts, the peaks of which had hardened and strained against the cotton of her T-shirt under his gaze, her previously flat belly which was now swollen sufficiently with his baby that her once loose-fitting top now skimmed it as she nervously shifted from one foot to the other.

His gaze drifted up from those feet and his groin tightened at the almost physical memory of those long, perfectly toned legs wrapped around his hips as she'd levered herself against him in the height of passion. And his chest constricted with the knowledge that in the midst of the most incredible night of his life he and this woman had created a child.

As a teenager Amanda-Jayne Vaughan had been his fantasy; four months ago fate had presented him with the opportunity to fulfil that fantasy. In those few brief hours of passion, fate and fantasy had combined to complicate whatever vague plans he'd had for his future—certainly marriage and fatherhood hadn't been among them—yet for some inexplicable reason the only decision he regretted was lying silent as she'd gathered her clothes and fled his hotel room.

For him the night had been magic and he refused to believe she had no recollection of what had happened between them.

Every brain cell in Amanda-Jayne's head urged her to run. But they were drowned out by the loud thumping of her heart and her body's inability to acknowledge anything but the soundless, sensual intent of Reb's eyes. She was as helpless to look away from the hungry desire they focused on her as she was to ignore the fiery sensuality snaking through every fibre of her being. Speech was beyond her, but considering the state of her mind that was probably a blessing; the wild images it had initially conjured had suddenly turned into wilful, wanton wishes which, if voiced aloud, would have shocked her conscience and perhaps changed her mind. *And she didn't want to change her mind.* Rightly or wrongly she wanted to make love with this man whose eyes were transmitting his thoughts to her body as effectively as his words or touch could have; more effectively. Had she been a guitar his eyes could have strummed her to song. Had she been ice his glance would have melted her. And had she been frightened his gaze would have instilled bravery.

Her breath came out in a rush as he reduced the distance between them with slow, determined strides.

Her words came out as a moan as his fingers ploughed into her hair and tilted her head back.

And her response came out as a gratified groan as his arousal pressed against her belly...

The intensity of their combined heat caused her vision to haze, but she met his gaze without blinking.

'How much of that night do you remember?' he demanded, his voice rasping.

The underlying desperation in his voice dragged the truth from her. 'Too much for me to deal with then.'

'How much?' he pushed, one hand palming her buttocks to draw her nearer.

'All of it,' she whispered, arching into him. 'I remember all of it...'

Uttering a murmured prayer, he swooped on her mouth, claiming it with a fevered passion that both matched and increased Amanda-Jayne's own. Long moments later, he scooped her into his arms and carried her to the bedroom.

Not trusting his desire-weakened knees to keep him upright a second longer, Reb lowered her to the ground inside the door and turned to lock it. His breath caught as her knuckles slowly grazed the indentation of his spine from the base of his neck to the towel riding his hips. With nothing more than a light tug it fell to his ankles.

He spun around in time to catch the surprise of her action still reflected in her own eyes, but it was superseded so quickly by a look of such pure feminine appreciation that Reb almost choked on his ego.

'You're beautiful.'

Her words were a shy, breathy whisper, but the touch of her fingers low on his belly jolted him from his bemused stupor. Seizing the hem of her T-shirt with both hands, he pulled it off and tossed it aside in one motion.

'So,' he said roughly, in a voice he didn't recognise as his own, 'are you.'

Amanda-Jayne shivered with a curious blend of fear, pleasure and anticipation as he placed the heel of his hand

at the base of her sternum, before gently gliding it down-
wards. Conscious that her stomach was no longer flat, she
immediately tried to suck it in.

'*Don't,*' he said, his voice as firm as his touch was light,
his eyes swimming with desire. 'I want you exactly as you
are now.'

It was as much the effect of the evocative admission as
the request itself that had her breath gushing from her and
her hands grabbing at his forearms to keep her steady, as
his hand continued its downward caress and his eyes continued to bore into hers.

'I want to make love to the mother of my child,' he went
on, his voice and hands both getting hypnotically lower.
'And know she's not resentful of that child. Or of me.'

'I'm not!' Passion and truth mangled her voice into a
throaty cry. He smiled, but he gave no chance for further
avowal.

'I want,' he said, his fingers delving through the tangle
of curls towards the damp heat he had created—a heat
which continued to build with every word he uttered, every
movement of his hand, every brush of his lips against her
throat— 'I want,' he repeated raggedly, 'to know that you
want me as much as I want you...'

His fingers continued to torture her mind by insidiously
dallying at the feminine heart of her with a promise it cruelly refused to deliver. A promise of the one thing which
would bring the release she craved.

'Tell me, babe,' he cajoled, against her ear, his other
hand massaging her buttocks. 'I want to know how much
you want me.'

More than my next breath, her body screamed, but the
affirmation stalled in her throat at the thought of how much
power she was giving him; how much of her emotions she
was exposing. She was suddenly unsure of herself, her desire fighting with her pride; a sob rose in her throat and she
buried her face in his shoulder to muffle it. But in that
instant that the realisation registered his body was trem-

bling more fiercely than her own, banishing her fears and replacing them with a heady joy.

It wasn't some macho power play that was prompting Reb to demand verbal declarations of her desire for him...it wasn't ego. It was *disbelief*. He didn't just want to hear her admit to the sexual attraction he held for her, he *needed* to hear it!

That knowledge simultaneously made her feel more vulnerable and yet stronger and more confident than anything else ever could have. Spurred on by a heady sense of sensual freedom she'd only ever felt with him but subsequently had pushed from her mind out of a misplaced sense of shame, she seized his head in her hands and claimed his mouth in a sizzling kiss. She wanted to test out her new confidence, to make *him tell her* exactly how much he wanted her...

But somewhere along the way she lost focus of her objective, got caught up in the flavour that was uniquely him, became distracted by the tiny sparks that the touch of his hand against her breasts sent showering into her belly. The tiny mews of delight he elicited from her as his tongue mated with hers, his throaty growls as her teeth tested the texture of his muscular shoulders, knitted with their erratic breathing pattern to form the most erotic symphony she'd ever heard.

Under his skilful handling, her arousal spiralled higher and higher, her internal organs growing hotter and hotter until she was slicked with sweat inside and out. Passion fogged her thoughts, desire and lust clouded her memory and she forgot everything but the 'Bad Boy' in her arms. The man who'd fulfilled her beyond her wildest imaginings; the man who'd given her the child she'd thought she'd never have.

Reb gave up trying to stay in control. He hadn't been able to that night in Sydney and he knew he didn't have a hope now. This woman held a power he couldn't rise above. With all except her he'd been able to maintain his sense of self, the knowledge that his desire wasn't ungovernable, the certainty that when the mutual lust was spent nothing in his life would be changed. He'd been Amanda-Jayne's lover for just a few hours yet in that time his entire future had been re-routed. Now she was his wife and the mother of his child… To love her again was, he suspected, to put his heart, perhaps his very soul, at risk. But God help him…he didn't give a damn!

Though his emotional strength was all but gone, physically it was no effort to lift her against him, yet as her legs wrapped around him the shudder his body gave made him grateful for the support of the door against his shoulders. It was then, in that indefinable space of time between settling her damp core against him and taking what at this moment he needed more than life itself, that she lifted her head to stare at him through desire-smoky eyes and whispered something that lit his inner uncertainty with a spark of hope…

'I want you, Reb… Only you…'

Amanda-Jayne supposed that the total absence of 'morning after' awkwardness she felt as Reb stirred to wakefulness beside her was due partly to the fact that it was after midday and partly because of the passion and intimacy of their lovemaking. Then again, she thought wryly, considering she'd just discovered a wonderful new flexibility she hadn't guessed she possessed it was probably only logical 'awkward' was the last word she'd be apt to apply to herself or should expect to be feeling.

So what *was* she feeling? Bemused? Stunned? Amazed? *Satiated beyond her wildest dreams?*

Well, yes. All of those things. But she was also feeling that maybe her marriage had a brighter future than she would have credited to it as recently as this morning. It wasn't just the incredible sex they'd shared which had her thinking along these lines, although Lord knew Reb's prowess in that department could turn a woman's head inside out! No, what had really surprised her was the intangible…well, the intangible *connection*, she supposed, that she'd experienced in his arms.

It would have been easy to attribute that to a bond provided by their unborn child, but to do so would have been to lie to herself again. The connection she'd felt with Reb today had been exactly the same one which had sent her fleeing from his bed under the cover of darkness four months ago. Now, however, the bed they shared was flooded in sunlight and the consequences of that long-ago night prevented her from running from the situation. In fact she wasn't sure she'd have run even if she could have, or indeed had somewhere to go.

What woman in her right mind would leave a man who not only was the most incredible lover she'd ever had, but who showed her more tenderness and consideration than anyone she'd ever known? Reb's constant enquiries as to what gave *her* pleasure, what was and wasn't safe for the baby, had revealed a thoughtfulness and concern she'd never expected. All her life she'd been *told* she was special, but no one—at least no one who didn't have anything to gain financially from her or her family—had ever treated her that way. Until Reb Browne.

The dreamy sigh that escaped her was unintentional but loud enough to have the man beside her up on one elbow and giving her a smug, teasing smile.

'You sound and look very well satisfied. Any particular reason?'

She grinned. 'I could say the exact same of you,' she said, feeling immensely proud that she was capable of not just exciting but satisfying a man like him. 'What's got *you* looking so wonderfully cheerful?'

'Oh, just that it's occurred to me that my petrol expenditure is going to be greatly reduced from now on.'

Now there was a reality check! Talk about pride going before the fall!

'Oh,' she said, now having to force her smile. 'That's nice.'

'Mmm,' he agreed. 'That pampered blue toy you call a car won't go through near as much juice now that you'll have other things to do in the middle of the night when you can't sleep, instead of taking those long, aimless drives alone.'

Amanda-Jayne's world immediately shifted back into its perfect place and took her heart with it.

'You know,' he continued in a conversational tone, 'I reckon it's a toss-up whether those nocturnal excursions have cost me more in lost sleep and worry or in dollars.'

'Well, then, I've got an idea as to how to solve the problem of your worry. We could take those drives together. You'd still be out of pocket and short of sleep,' she said, drawing a fingernail lightly across his jaw, 'but I've always been curious about what it would be like to make love in a car.'

'*Witch!*' Reb groaned, and rolled onto his back, taking her with him. 'But I'm sorry, you'll just have to stay curious,' he murmured against her mouth. ''Cos a lady like you deserves a whole lot better than that.'

Amanda-Jayne wanted to argue the point, but not as much as she wanted to continue kissing him…

CHAPTER EIGHT

'GEE, Reb, did you leave the cat *any* cream? I've never seen you so happy about changing a head gasket.'

'We don't have a cat, Savvy.'

'We don't have much in the way of a pantry any more either,' his cousin replied, handing him the spanner he wordlessly requested with nothing more than an outstretched hand. 'I think you need to tell your wife that, while we appreciate her cordon-bleu cooking, groceries don't replenish themsclvcs.'

Reb straightened from his bent position over the engine, worried that the fragile truce A.J. and Savvy seemed to have established in the last few weeks was in danger of shattering at his feet. Since the consummation of their marriage, A.J. seemed to be a lot more relaxed and tolerant towards everything and everyone, but particularly his young cousin. Reb had to admit that he wasn't finding it a whole lot of hardship being married to Amanda-Jayne Vaughan; she was talented in the kitchen, even more so in the bedroom, and creative in both. When a man had his two biggest appetites so well nourished he'd be greedy to ask for anything else.

Wouldn't he?

Uncomfortable with the wandering direction of his thoughts, he shifted them to his cousin.

'I thought you both just came back from shopping,' he said.

Savannah rolled her eyes, the action causing Reb to notice her make-up was noticeably underdone compared to her usual standards.

'We did,' she said. 'But A.J.'s idea of grocery shopping

is so frugal I figure the Vaughans made all their money starving themselves! I mean it, Reb,' she said when he laughed. 'I put two packets of chocolate biscuits into the trolley and she took them out, saying they weren't a necessity.'

'Obviously she hasn't noticed the link between you, PMS and chocolate withdrawal,' he teased.

'Well, I hope you hang onto your sense of humour when you find yourself drinking *powdered* orange juice in the morning instead of the real thing. And when you discover the tomato sauce you've smothered your sausages in is that cheap generic brand you hate.'

'*Sausages?* Aw, Savvy, I loathe sausages, you know that!'

'According to A.J. that's only because you haven't tasted hers.' She shrugged. 'Personally I'll eat just about anything so long as I can have my supply of my chocolate bickies, but I have to warn you…things could get ugly if I suddenly have to go cold turkey on them. And—' Three sharp blasts of a car horn had her turning towards the entrance of the workshop. 'Oh, gosh, Kara and her mum are here; gotta go!'

Reb frowned even as he recognised the car. 'Go *where*, exactly?'

Again he was treated to the rolling-eyes routine. 'To Kara's sister Michelle's place. We're baby-sitting while she's studying at tech, remember?'

'Oh, right. How are you getting home?'

'I'm not. I'm staying the night.'

'At Kara's?'

'*At her sister's.* Geez, Reb, I told you this once already. Where has A.J. got you keeping your mind these days?'

Reb ignored the leading question. 'What about your homework?'

'It's in the bag!' Grinning, she patted her shoulder satchel. 'See ya!'

Satisfied there was no reason to say she couldn't go, he

grunted approval, adding to her rapidly departing back, 'Be careful. And phone if there's a crisis.'

'Yeah, phone anyone but Reb,' Debbie tossed in, crossing from the office. 'His idea of getting a kid to stop cryin' and co-operate is to bribe them with sugar.'

'There's no law that says a man can't buy treats for his goddaughter occasionally,' he said in his defence, pulling a cigarette pack from the chest pocket of his overalls. 'Matter of fact I think it's mandatory.'

'Married life must be gettin' to you,' Debbie said dryly. 'You're smokin' more than ever these days.'

'No, I'm smoking less,' he said, bypassing the solitary cigarette in the packet and extracting a foil of nicotine gum from beside it. He unwrapped it and popped it into his mouth, grinning smugly. 'A.J. asked me not to smoke upstairs on account of the effects of passive smoking on the baby so if I am desperate the only chance I get to light up is when I'm down here.'

'Well, whoopee for Saint A.J.! My smokin' never did Alanna any harm.' The aggressive tone of the response set Reb's teeth on edge.

'As I recall, Debbie,' he said tightly, 'New Year's Eve you claimed Alanna was the reason *you* were determined to kick the habit this time. So by rights you should be applauding A.J.'s actions, not sneering at them.'

The blonde head dipped to the invoices she held. 'About these bills—'

'Forget the bills for the time being,' he said. 'I want to know why you're having such a hard time accepting A.J. Gunna seems to be getting on with her well enough.'

'Gunna, like most men, thinks with his—'

'*Do not go there, Debbie!*' he cut in harshly. 'This is my wife we're speaking about here. *And*, I might add, *your partner.*'

The petite blonde had the grace to look shamefaced.

'Now, how about you tell me what your real problem

with A.J. is? 'Cos it's getting way too hard for me to ignore it any longer.'

'I don't— No, damn it! If you must know, I think she's the greatest snob on two legs! I think she's suckered you big time and that even though you're in sex heaven right now in the end she's going to break your heart.'

Reb sighed, debating how to respond. He had his own theories on the heartbreak bit, but since he'd avoided examining them too closely himself he sure wasn't going to air them publicly. As for who'd suckered whom… *He* was the one keeping secrets. A.J. had at least taken him at face value, whereas he'd hired an investigator to probe her personal and financial life. But that was something only he and A.J. knew about and, while he'd had his reasons for doing what he did, these days he was sufficiently ashamed of his actions not to want anyone else to know. So where did that leave him…?

'Of course A.J. is a snob,' he heard himself say. 'Her father spent a fortune sending her to expensive schools and deportment and elocution classes that mastered in snobbery. In fact she has scads of certificates to *prove* she's a snob…' He couldn't stifle a smile as he paraphrased A.J.'s words to him. Although he doubted he'd looked quite as surprised hearing them from A.J. as Debbie did when they sprouted from him.

'As for her legs…' He winked. 'I'd argue they're the best you'd find anywhere.'

Debbie despairingly shook her head. 'I swear, Reb, I'd be less worried about you if someone produced proof your body had been taken over by aliens.'

'Trouble with you, Deb, is you read too much Stephen King. But how about you do me a favour…? Lighten up on A.J., okay?'

The muscles at the side of her mouth momentarily pinched before she said, 'Fine. As long as you keep her out of *my* office. I'll take orders from you, but I'll quit before

I take them from her, because your *certified snob* doesn't know a spark plug from a fan belt.'

Reb grinned. 'I know that. Trust me, I'm not going to suddenly make her head mechanic.'

'Maybe not, but you haven't done anything to discourage her from coming in here every day with her "Can I do anything to help you, Debbie?" act.'

Reb couldn't deny being aware of the fact that A.J. had started venturing into the garage more often of late. Truth be told, he was so constantly aware of her whenever she was in the garage, his pulse practically logged her time of arrival to the second, the number of breaths she took while she was here and the precise time she left! But he hadn't known she'd been offering to help out around the place. He wasn't sure what to make of that, but he doubted she had any sinister intent to take over.

'C'mon, Deb, she's probably bored with nothing to occupy her. In Sydney she would've had an active social life and—'

'Bet that gave her blisters.'

'*Debbie*… Look, surely you can find her something uncomplicated to do. Couldn't you just let her answer the phone or something?'

'She did yesterday. And when Lou Abrahams asked if the part for his new two-stroke was in she told him we were a garage and he should call a lawnmower shop!'

Amusement and surprise warred inside Reb. 'Well, there you go!' he said with theatrical triumph. 'Evidence that she shows mechanical promise. You and I know bikes come in two- and four-stroke varieties, but not many women from her background could be expected to know lawnmowers have two-stroke motors.'

'Oh, I give up! You'd find a way of excusin' her actions if she stormed the council chambers with an AK47 and took the mayor hostage,' Debbie grumbled, shoving the invoices she held in his face. 'Here, what do you want me to do about these bills? There are two dozen of them and they're all overdue by at least sixty days.'

Reb scanned the names on the top of the invoices. He knew that with the exception of three regularly delinquent accounts none of the other long-time customers were in a position to pay their bills. Many had been unemployed since the saw mill closed eight months ago, some longer.

With a resigned sigh, he handed the papers back to Debbie. 'Can't get blood out of a stone, kiddo. Guess we'll just have to let them slide for another month.'

'That's what I figured you'd say,' Debbie said. 'Okay. I'll be getting back to the statements, then... Oh, by the way I need a couple of cheques signed before I leave; I wanna post 'em on the way home.'

'Since I'm intending to take an early mark, I better come and do it now. Listen, did Gunna happen to say how long he'd be at...?'

As quietly as she could Amanda-Jayne turned and hurried back to the apartment from her position halfway down the stairs. She hadn't meant to eavesdrop, but Debbie's scathing reference to her had momentarily frozen her to the spot. They said eavesdroppers never heard good of themselves, but obviously they sometimes heard a whole lot more than they'd expected...

'Reb, are you planning to have a party?' she asked as he paused in row ten of the supermarket and added several varieties of corn chips to an already cramped shopping trolley.

'No. Why?'

'Because there's no way you, Savvy and myself will possibly get through this much junk food in a week.'

'I know. But with luck it should save you having to shop for anything except meat and vegetables for at least a month. Now, what else do we need?' he mused aloud. 'Oh, right, orange juice.'

'I bought orange juice when I came here earlier today.'

'No, you bought that concentrated rubbish. Which I can't stand and doesn't have enough vitamin C left in it to be of any use to a pregnant woman.'

Amanda-Jayne stopped herself from pointing out she was already on a vitamin supplement; the announcement would probably only encourage him to rush back to the health food section and grab forty bottles of the stuff and the mental tab she was keeping was already rocketing worryingly high. While it was *his* money he was spending, not for the first time she wished there were some way she could relieve some of the additional financial burden the circumstances of their marriage was putting on Reb. In the past she'd always spent a lavish sum on her lingerie, but the cost of the three maternity bras she'd had no choice but to buy earlier today had suddenly seemed criminal—and not merely because their ugliness offended her sense of taste.

When she'd married Reb she hadn't given much thought to his financial situation except to acknowledge that what it had cost him to clear her debts would have put a large dent in his cheque book, but she'd assumed that if he'd not been well ahead of financial insolvency he wouldn't have done it. Now, in view of what she'd observed these past weeks and what she'd inadvertently overheard today, she had a horrible feeling that solvency for the Browne Bike and Auto Emporium was very much a day-to-day proposition. It was therefore an enormous relief that when they reached the checkout Reb not only produced sufficient cash to pay for the goods, but also a discount card; she just wished it had occurred to her to use hers today—

Her thoughts came to a screeching halt. *What was Reb doing with a card issued only when people bought a certain number of shares in the nationwide company?*

'How'd you get that card?' she asked more aggressively than she intended. 'Only shareholders get those!'

'Oh, no, staff get them too!' the teenaged checkout operator butted in without pausing in her scanning of the goods. 'Cool, huh?'

Amanda-Jayne opened her mouth to argue that Reb wasn't staff, but he apparently read her thoughts.

'I've got the tender to supply the petrol and mechanical maintenance for the company's trucks in this region,' he said. Then, after instructing the cashier to have the packed groceries sent to the customer pick-up bay, he took Amanda-Jayne's elbow and steered her to the mall exit and out into the street.

Despite the fact the days were still mimicking the last of summer, the early evening air was embracing autumn and the dress of Thursday night shoppers of Vaughan's Landing reflected both seasons.

'Anything special you have to do?'

She shook her head. 'I did all my personal shopping today.' Again the cost of the bras pinched her conscience, even though she'd passed the point of where their purchase could have been called premature weeks ago. Secretly she suspected it was the sheer novelty of having breasts large enough to spill over the top of her normal A cup which had had her postponing the purchase this long, but finally comfort had won out over vanity.

Caught up in her own inane thoughts, she took a moment to realise they weren't heading back to where Reb had parked the four-by-four.

'Where are we going?'

'Eventually…somewhere to eat,' Reb told her, snaring her close to his body and out of the way of danger as two boys appeared from nowhere to make a kamikaze-like run at them on skateboards. 'But Savvy's been going on and on at me about letting her go to the year twelve social next term and dropping subtle hints that she wants a new dress—'

'Subtle isn't a word I immediately associate with Savvy,' she cut in dryly.

Reb frowned. 'She still giving you a hard time?'

'Oh, no,' Amanda-Jayne said hastily, then amended her

comment with, 'Not *really*. I just meant that she usually isn't backward in coming forward.'

'True. But by hints I meant she's been making obscure comments such as how everyone always says she looks fabulous in black and then suggesting I really should take a look at the renovations they've done to Murphy's hardware store,' he said wryly.

'So?' Amanda-Jayne frowned. 'I don't get the connection…'

'Think,' Reb said. 'What's right next door to Murphy's?'

'Aha!' she exclaimed on a chuckle as she mentally turned the corner ahead and saw the hardware store flanked by a newsagency and a boutique. 'Hey, you're sharper than you look,' she teased. 'I wouldn't have picked up on a hint that subtle.'

'Oh, I was on the receiving end of a heap more,' he said dryly. 'But, to condense it into something resembling lucidity, the particular dress she wants should leap out from the display and grab me by the throat. Since I doubt very much it will I'm going to be relying on your female instincts to help me out.'

'Dream on!' Amanda-Jayne laughed. 'Like Savvy and I have even *remotely* similar tastes! Wouldn't it be easier if you just came shopping with her?'

Reb stopped dead and shot her a horrified look. 'I'd sooner perform microsurgery and she'd rather be the patient.'

Their light-hearted banter continued until they reached the boutique, but nothing hanging in the artfully arranged window immediately snagged Amanda-Jayne's attention. What *did* was a notice taped in the bottom right-hand corner of the glass.

POSITION VACANT!
PART-TIME SALES ASSISTANT REQUIRED WITHIN
NO EXPERIENCE NECESSARY,
BUT MUST BE WELL GROOMED WITH A COURTEOUS
MANNER.

Feeling as if she were Cinderella and her fairy godmother had just zapped a pumpkin into a coach, she struggled to contain her excitement. She wanted to rush into the store and speak with the manager right away, but the voice of pessimism reminded her that given her previous track record in endeavouring to secure employment she ran the risk of embarrassing herself. The last person she wanted to witness her being told she wasn't qualified to handle the job was Reb, who'd more or less told her he regarded her as spoilt and pampered to the extent of being almost completely useless. Oh, he mightn't have used those exact words or suggested it recently, but that didn't stop her from wanting to change his opinion of her. And in fact this time it was her spoilt, pampered past which made her eminently qualified for the advertised position; one thing she knew her way around was a dress shop! Co-ordinating, mixing 'n' matching and accessorising was stuff she could do in her sleep; the only difference was this time she'd be doing it for the benefit of someone else and getting paid for it.

'There is no way in hell I'd consider buying *that* for her.'

She jumped at the harsh intrusion of Reb's voice, her gaze following his viciously jabbed finger to a slinky black beaded dress. After a quick glance to assess the other garments on display Amanda-Jayne decided that since this was the only black one it presumably was the one Savvy had been talking about. It was, however, nothing like the dress she'd pictured the girl wanting.

'I…er…take it,' she ventured, 'you don't like it.'

'For heaven's sake, A.J., Savvy's a *schoolgirl*. She's going to a school dance, not the Academy Awards. What they're charging for that minuscule piece of fabric would keep every girl her age in uniforms for the next three years!'

Reb was exaggerating in the extreme, but again guilt prickled down her spine. She doubted she owned anything other than a few T-shirts which had come in under the dress's three-figure price tag. 'Under the circumstances I guess it is a bit much,' she said aloud.

'A *bit* much? It's way too much. Too much of everything except dress,' he muttered.

Giving the window one last baleful glare, he snared her hand. 'C'mon, maybe my good mood will return if I get some food into my stomach. Let's head to Captains.'

'*Captains?* Dressed like this?' Her eyes took in their blue jeans and bulky sweaters.

'It specialises in seafood, we're wearing fishermen's sweaters…' He shrugged. 'Doesn't get any more appropriate than that in my book.'

She burst out laughing. 'You're incorrigible! Even if we had a reservation we'd be lucky to get past the door looking like this.'

'Then we'll have to hope our luck is good…' He grinned and flicked her nose. ''Cos it just so happens we *do* have reservations. In the name of Browne. For…' he checked his watch… 'ten minutes from now. Which is a good thing because I'm starving.'

She should have argued that Captains was too expensive, that they could be home in fifteen minutes and that she didn't mind cooking. But she didn't…for two reasons. One was that he was looking so adorably pleased with himself… The other was because her heart was bouncing with joy and her mind kept flashing, *First Date! First Date!*

Reb knew that, after looking him up and down, the *maître d'* was on the verge of bouncing him out of the place, before Amanda-Jayne moved into the guy's line of vision and greeted him by name. Watching the guy's superior attitude slide to perplexed confusion made Reb smile, but mere moments later he found himself struggling to stifle a belly laugh when the tuxedo-clad idiot attempted to lead them to what was obviously the worst table in the place, and A.J. oh, so coolly informed him that since her step-

mother's favourite table was vacant they'd have *that* one.
With the restaurant practically empty, the waiter had no
way of graciously refusing her and the self-satisfied gleam
in her eye revealed how much she'd enjoyed outmanouevr-
ing the man.

The decor and the clientele backed up Captains' reputation as being the swankiest eatery within a fifty-kilometre
radius and Reb couldn't help feeling disappointed that,
without even consulting the menu, A.J. announced she only
wanted salad. He also wondered if he hadn't made a bad
choice when he mused aloud that he felt like lobster and
she looked aghast. But her reaction became clear when he
opened the menu and the absence of prices sent the silent
message that if you needed to know them you couldn't
afford to eat there. He smiled inwardly, suspecting he was
the first mechanic ever to darken Captains' doors.

'Relax, A.J.' He stilled her hand worrying the stem of
her water glass and her gaze instantly rose to meet his. 'I
promise you won't have to wash the dishes. Not only do I
suspect they have a dishwasher, but I wouldn't have
brought you here if I couldn't afford to pay the bill.'

She blushed. 'I…er…this just seems a bit extravagant.'

He lifted one eyebrow to give her his most sceptical look.
'You're not going to try and tell me you're uncomfortable,
are you? Because I won't buy it. You're on a first-name
basis with the *maître d'*.'

'It's not me I'm feeling uncomfortable for,' she retorted.
'I'm surprised you aren't bleeding to death from the number of daggers that went into your back as we walked in.'

Her indignation on his behalf made him want to dive
across the table and kiss her senseless. He limited himself
to just lifting her hand and kissing her palm.

'As much as I appreciate your concern,' he said, pleased
with the flush his innocent kiss brought to her cheeks, 'I've
survived twenty-seven years of daggered looks from the
people in this town; a few more won't finish me off.

'Now.' He smiled. 'Do you think you can sit back, stop

worrying about what everyone is thinking and just enjoy the evening? Apart from a meal at a truck stop this is the first time we've shared a table alone.'

Looking pleased and mischievous, she reclaimed her hand and sat back in her chair. 'All right, but you better signal the waiter... I've decided I don't want just salad after all.'

From that point on they became oblivious to everything and everyone around them, their conversation ceasing only when the waiter brought their meals. They discussed everything from their opposing political beliefs to their favourite colours, but, while Reb initially claimed he didn't have one, as the night sped on he found himself thinking that he had several... The copper of her hair, the precise brown of her eyes, the sunshine-gold of her laughter.

He still wasn't sure what had possessed him to phone and make the reservation here when he'd finished work, but suddenly it seemed like the third smartest idea he'd ever had. Ahead of it was the dead heat of taking her back to his hotel that night and marrying her. Yet even while things between them were better than he'd imagined they would be—to his mind getting better and better every day—he was still caught up in the internal debate of how honest he could afford to be with her.

Maybe *that* was subconsciously why he'd brought her here... She'd seemingly been fitting so contentedly into his lifestyle that he wanted to see if sudden re-exposure to the rarefied existence she'd known before would cause her to regress. The notion was enough to make him feel guilty, but not enough to overlook that she'd done nothing to indicate she envisaged the possibility that their marriage would stretch beyond the agreed three-year term. How would she respond to an outright question on the possibility? he wondered.

The temptation to call her on it was strong, but the fear of having her laugh in his face was stronger. He'd rather have her under false pretences than find her true colours weren't as attractive as those she currently flew.

Oh, who was he trying to kid? Even back when he hadn't seen anything that argued against her cold, rich-bitch reputation, he'd wanted her with a need that sent him hard in his sleep. These past months might have exposed a warmer, more sensitive and decidedly more vulnerable side of Amanda-Jayne Vaughan to him, but the truth was his need for her was such that, be she saint or sinner, the thought of losing her chilled him to his soul.

'Can I ask you a personal question?' Though her voice was soft it had no trouble triumphing over his rowdy, disturbing thoughts.

He nodded seriously. 'I think wives and lovers are allowed to do that.'

She pertly wrinkled her nose before saying, 'I was wondering how you came to be Savvy's legal guardian...'

'I'd have thought the town grapevine would've made that common knowledge by now.'

Her shoulders rose in a dismissive shrug. 'The last nine years I've only come to Vaughan's Landing to fulfil the obligations and expectations my dual role of perfect daughter and town princess required.' The self-deprecating statement was accompanied by a wry smile. 'The last gossip I heard about the town's resident Bad Boy was that he'd left town after getting arrested in a pub brawl.'

'He did. But he came back five years ago when his uncle was killed in a bike accident and his ten-year-old cousin was going to be made a state ward.' The genuine concern and interest in her silent appraisal encouraged him to continue.

'Savvy's mother hadn't been heard of since she walked out when Sav was a toddler. Having done stints in state-run institutions myself as a kid, there was no way I was going to let Savvy be put into one so I filed for guardianship. My uncle had taken me in when my old man crucified himself on a syringe; I figured I owed him.'

The pallor of her face made him wish he hadn't phrased things quite so brutally, so he hurried to finish the story and end the discussion.

'By rights my father should have left his share of the garage to my uncle—he was the one who kept it going—but it came to me.' He sighed. 'Bill died while I was off racing bikes and busting limbs. With him gone and Savvy only a kid I came back and took over running things. And here we are.'

For a moment she simply stared at him, then one of those smiles that made him feel like the greatest man ever born edged across her face. 'I hope Savvy appreciates how very lucky she was to have you. Not many guys in their early twenties would have assumed the responsibility you did. It can't have been easy dealing with an orphaned ten-year-old.'

'You reckon? Looking back it seems a damned sight easier than dealing with the fifteen-year-old wild child she is now. Get this,' he said. 'She's already got more holes in her ears than a sieve and now she wants to get her *eyebrow* pierced.'

Amanda-Jayne struggled with a grin. 'Yes, I know.'

'Huh! Probably approached you to soften me up, did she?'

'Er, no. I overheard the discussion you and she were having in the garage the other night. On her part at least it was very…er…loud and impassioned.' She bit her lip, no longer able to rein in her amusement. 'I don't think I even knew those words existed when I was her age.'

Reb groaned. 'Savvy's too street-wise for her own good. Not that it's her fault. She's hardly had a conventional up-bringing, but since mine was as bad if not worse it's a case of the blind trying to lead the blind.'

'Stop being so hard on yourself, Reb. It's not like she's out of control. Basically she seems pretty…er…normal, compared to most of her friends.'

'Her friends are half the problem.' He gave an exasperated sigh. 'How do I convince her that she deserves a better future than she's setting herself up for without encouraging the idea she's better than everyone else?'

'I...I don't know. We can't help being products of our environment, Reb. I know that better than most people, I guess. But fourteen months ago when I finally bit the bullet and left Anthony I think I took the first step away from being a slave to mine. Savvy—'

'What do you mean?' he said, not willing to let the first reference she'd made to her former marriage slide by. 'Why'd you leave?'

She traced several figure eights on the table cloth before lifting her head. 'I married Anthony during my second year of an art degree at Sydney University. But make no mistake,' she said, her eyes narrowing, 'it wasn't expected I would graduate with a degree. The arts courses the Vaughan women traditionally undertake are regarded as Marriage Hunt Year 1, Year 2 and Year 3. The fact my aunt graduated with honours and a Ph.D. has always been blamed on the fact she was the ugly duckling of the family.'

She drew a long breath before continuing.

'Anthony swept me off my feet and also impressed the life out of everyone who met him in the process. He was good-looking, ambitious and well bred; everyone from my father to the society columnists regarded our union as *the* match of the century. When everyone was telling me how lucky I was to have him, it was hard to worry about the fact he was going through my trust money. Mind you,' she said dryly, 'it was somewhat harder *not* to worry when rumours started flying that he was ''going through'' my so-called friends as well.'

'He was cheating on you?'

'He didn't see it that way. According to him my abysmally poor sexual prowess was cheating him out of the physical satisfaction a married man should receive from his wife.'

Rage erupted so violently within him that Reb was certain the top of his head was plastered to the ceiling. 'And you *believed* that pile of—'

'It was difficult not to, Reb. Any hints I dropped to my father that his golden-haired boy was being less than faithful to me were regarded as…well, if not my imagination, then certainly my fault. I was reminded also that no matter what the circumstances the Vaughans had never sullied themselves with something as middle class as divorce—the fatherly message clearly being I should either pick up my game or have the dignity to turn a blind eye.'

Reb swore under his breath. And people reckoned *he* came from a dysfunctional family!

'It was after one of these futile visits with my father that I returned to Sydney and walked in on Anthony and his boss's wife. That's when I decided that since I couldn't live up to other people's expectations of me I'd better at least try and live up to my own. I told Anthony to lock up when he left, walked out of the apartment and on the way to the family solicitors to instigate divorce proceedings I called Anthony's boss on my car phone and told him where to find his wife.' Her wry smile turned into a sigh. 'Needless to say it was a long, ugly, drawn-out court battle and my father died before it was final… I'd like to think that in the end he'd forgiven me, but…'

'For God's sake you'd done nothing to forgive!' Reb said, wanting to shake her. 'Hell, A.J., right now I don't know who I'm more furious with—your idiot of an ex, your pompous, insensitive father or you for believing the garbage they fed you!'

That he should be so outraged on her behalf touched her deeply, but she hated the fact that he was again drawing darts of disapproval from around the restaurant. She didn't want an ugly scene to ruin the wonderful night they'd shared.

'Shh,' she urged, her hand closing over his. 'People can hear you.'

'I couldn't give a stuff!' he retorted, sliding from his

chair to crouch before hers. 'Just so long as *you* hear, listen and comprehend everything I'm about to say… So,' he said, gently cradling her face. 'Are you listening?'

With his nearness and the intensity of his dark eyes nullifying her vocal cords Amanda-Jayne nodded, but she didn't think she'd hear anything over the drumming of her heart.

'You,' he said, his gaze never deviating from hers, his thumbs lightly grazing her cheekbones, 'you are the most incredibly sexy, beautiful and sensual woman I've ever known…'

His words came out in a rasped whisper that brushed her face more lightly than a breeze, yet caught at her emotions with the force of a tornado.

'Your ex was a jerk,' he continued. 'It wasn't your money that compelled me to take you to my hotel that night. It isn't the thought of your money which turns me on every time I look at you. And it sure isn't an economical decision which has me praying you'll agree to pass on dessert so we can get out of this place!'

The tears in Amanda-Jayne's eyes made her uncertain if he'd lowered his lips to hers or if she'd risen to initiate their kiss, but ultimately it didn't matter; all that did was that this man made her feel more special than any other living soul.

'Does that mean you want to skip dessert?' Reb asked, easing back from her bone-melting response to his kiss.

A slow, sly smile slipped across her lips. 'No…' she said, slowly drawing a finger across his lower lip, seduction blazing in her eyes. 'Just that I'd rather have it at home.'

Reb snatched out his wallet, drew out a wad of bills and fisted them, before scooping A.J. from her chair.

Her surprised squeal ensured every head in the place swung in their direction. 'Reb, you idiot! Put me down!'

Because she was obviously more amused than embarrassed he ignored her request and started towards the door. Laughing, she buried her head in his shoulder and whispered, 'You realise you're likely to send the other patrons into shock, don't you?'

'Honey, they'd get more of a shock if you *weren't* camouflaging the front of my jeans.'

As they approached the horrified-looking *maître d'* Reb held the money towards him. 'That ought to cover it, mate,' he said, tucking the bills in the guy's top pocket when he remained statue-still with his jaw in the vicinity of his shoes. 'If not…well, I'm sure you know where to find me.'

Before the waiter had a chance to respond in any way, A.J.'s hand flashed out and pulled a twenty-dollar note back from the waiter's pocket. 'That's too much, Reb,' she said. 'The service doesn't warrant a tip.' She stared right at the *maître d'* as she added, 'For some inexplicable reason, tonight it was nowhere near the standard Captains usually affords me. I *won't* be coming back.'

Reb figured the tone of her voice should have reduced everything within a hundred-metre radius to ice, but knowing her ire stemmed from the undercurrent of disapproval directed at him all night filled him with a soothing warmth. Usually his pride made him resentful of anyone feeling the need to defend him, but having A.J. do it had the opposite effect… It had him feeling damned lucky that she was in his corner and, more importantly, in his life.

CHAPTER NINE

AMANDA-JAYNE cast a final glance over the carefully decorated table, wishing that Reb would hurry up and get home. He'd left twenty minutes ago to collect Savvy from her friend's house and after having kept her surprise to herself for over nine hours her excitement had fermented to a level where she could barely contain it. She couldn't help it…*she felt so damned proud of herself*! Her success today was going to change everything; from now on she'd no longer feel as if her existence around here was a total waste of space and oxygen.

Her pulse leapt at the growl of an approaching motorbike and, snatching up a pair of oven mitts, she set about transferring the ready meal to the table. Satisfied everything was as perfect as she could make it, given the limitations of durable rather than delicate dinnerware and mismatched cutlery, she smiled. At the sound of what could have been a herd of elephants stampeding up the internal stairs she turned and waited for the surprised expression her efforts would bring to Reb's handsome face.

It was Savvy who burst into the apartment first.

'You cow!' she screeched by way of greeting. 'You selfish, money-grubbing, snooty-nosed—'

'Savvy!' Reb followed on her heels, grabbing an arm that appeared to be swinging towards Amanda-Jayne. 'That's enough! Now settle down!'

'I won't settle down! I should've expected you'd take *her* side!'

'I'm not taking anyone's side, I'm still trying to get the full story.'

Reefing free of her cousin's grasp, she directed a look

130

of pure hate at Amanda-Jayne. 'The story *is*,' she said venomously, 'she's got heaps more money than anyone alive and she's still not satisfied!'

Staggered by Savvy's fury, she sent Reb a questioning glance. He returned it with an emotionless study of silent perusal.

'Wh-what have I done?' she stammered, scrambling to work out what was going on.

'As if you didn't know!' Savannah sneered.

'I...I don't.'

'Savvy said you applied for the sales job in the boutique.' Reb's statement wore as much disapproval as his overalls did grease and what remnants of the pleasure she'd been feeling a few moments ago instantly evaporated.

'Well?' he prodded. 'Did you or didn't you?'

Confusion as to why he was so obviously angry at the idea robbed her of words. It was all she could do to manage a nod.

'I told you so!' Savvy shouted, but Amanda-Jayne's attention was held transfixed by Reb's gaze.

'Would you mind telling me *why*?' he demanded of her.

'Because she's a selfish cow who thinks of no one but herself!'

'Savannah! Will you just shut up and let me deal with this?' Reb injected before Amanda-Jayne could formulate an answer to his question. She felt as if she'd been dropped into an episode of the *Twilight Zone*, where nothing was as it was supposed to be. She'd anticipated her success in getting the job would have inspired hearty congratulations and admiration; instead she was being subjected to scathing disapproval.

'A.J., I want to know what possessed you to apply for a job.'

'The same thing that possesses most people,' she retorted, confusion giving way to anger. 'I *wanted* one.'

'Why?' he insisted.

'Because I'm bored witless with nothing to do here every

day but sit around and get fat! I thought the money would come in handy! It's not like it's hard physical labour, Reb, if it's the baby you're worried about.'

'See, Reb! It's always got to be about her! It would never occur to you that there are people who need that job more than you do, would it?' The narrow-eyed glare Savvy nailed her with indicated the question wasn't rhetorical.

'I know a lot of people had applied for it, but obviously the owner didn't think they were as qualified for it as I was.'

'As *well connected*, you mean!' the teenager snapped. 'Michelle Costica, Kara's sister, was told the job was hers yesterday. Today she gets a phone call saying the owner had changed her mind.'

'I…I don't understand. That doesn't make sense; the notice was still in the window last night.'

'The store manager took it out first thing this morning, but when *you* phoned about an interview Michelle got the flick quick smart! Tell me,' she went on, 'did they even bother to interview you or was the Vaughan name and your country-club connections enough to seal things in your favour?'

'Look, Savvy, I don't know why the manager did what she did, but I certainly didn't pull any strings to get—'

'Oh, wake up to yourself, A.J.!' Reb cut into her defence in a ridiculing tone, angry fingers raking his hair. 'You didn't *have* to bother pulling strings. Your family name and the fact you've seemingly thumbed your nose at your blue-blooded heritage are the hottest bit of gossip this town has had in decades. Anyone with a scrap of nous knows you didn't get hired because of any so-called job skills you might have; your sole value to that store is as a crowd-puller for the cashed-up and curious.'

'Th-that's not fair!'

'No, it's not,' he agreed. 'Because for all you might feel like your current life isn't what it should be it's a damn sight better than most people's in this part of town! Unlike you, Michelle Costica doesn't come from a wealthy family or have a veritable fortune waiting for her when she turns thirty; her boyfriend's in gaol and she's fighting tooth and nail just to manage regular meals and keep a roof over her and her child's head. For *her* the money she'd have got from that job would've been a whole lot more than *handy*.'

The disappointment and disgust in his voice seared her to her soul. The tears welling in her eyes rose straight from her heart and her throat tightened into a hard, painful lump that prevented speech and restricted breathing. She'd expected him to shower her with praise; instead he'd rained on her parade more effectively than anyone else could have—a point Savvy's prolonged silence seemed to acknowledge.

'I wondered what all the cryptic comments I was getting today—about how things must be worse in the auto business than people thought—meant,' he continued. 'It never occurred to me that my *wife* was undermining my credibility as a provider! You wanna tell me how long you were planning to keep this a secret from me?'

She opened her mouth to—to what? Try and explain that she'd done it to help him, not hurt? What was the point? Once again he'd failed to give her actions the benefit of the doubt and she'd be damned if she'd chase his forgiveness when her intentions had only ever been well meaning! Forcing her chin up and her tears back, she kept her distance from him as she moved towards the bedroom.

'I'll phone the store owner and resign immediately; I'll also insist the job be given back to Kara's sister,' she informed them coolly. 'I assure you, however,' she went on in a formal tone that would have done credit to Patricia, 'it was *never* my intention to bring ridicule on the Browne name by applying for the position. But you're right, Reb,' she conceded, fighting to conceal the cracks in her fast crumbling façade. 'It *was* stupid of me to assume I might have been hired for my capabilities when history has proved all anyone has ever had use for is my *name*.'

Her words hit Reb like a punch to the guts and the expletive he uttered as she turned away came out as a hiss. 'A.J., wait! That's not what I meant.'

She spun back to him, her eyes too bright in her disbelieving face. 'It's what you said, Reb. Like everyone else you believe that because I'm a Vaughan I'm insensitive to the needs of others. That I've got and can get anything I've ever wanted by trading on my name. But you know what?' she said. 'There's one thing I always wanted and have *never* been able to get…and that's for people to look beyond my name, to look at *me* and either accept or reject me for the person I am, not for what my being a Vaughan can do for me. Or,' she added, 'for *them*.'

His speed was no match for the distance separating them and he reached the door only in time to feel the breeze created as she slammed it in his face. The sound of the bolt being thrown across it continued to reverberate through his entire body for hours.

No lights shone in the apartment when Reb returned five hours later. He immediately killed the motor and, knowing Lethal would wake the dead if he entered the apartment via the garage, he wheeled the bike around to the external stairs which led to the apartment balcony. The clear starry night held no threat of rain, but his concerns far outweighed those of what dew might do to the machine.

Sighing, he eased off his helmet and gloves, wishing he could claim the long, aimless ride had gone some way to clearing his head. It hadn't. And it hadn't made him feel any less of a jerk for the way he'd ripped into A.J. earlier either. He owed her an apology; he'd hurt her. The damnable thing was he'd hurt himself just as much in doing so. That was what had his head so badly scrambled; these days it was as if he was feeling everything through her. And what good was that going to do him if her stepmother, in a fit of conscience, released the money she was withholding and provided A.J. with the means to leave? Trapping her into marriage might have provided him with a legal hold on their unborn child, but he had no way of holding on to Amanda-Jayne.

He'd gone from thinking he held all the aces to finding he was the biggest joker of all time. The thought had him kicking the bike stand down more viciously than was necessary. Whatever way he looked at it, despite the fact he continually seemed to be making mistake after mistake where A.J. was concerned, and that her grace and poise made him achingly aware of his own shortcomings, she'd somehow become the most important thing in his life.

'Reb? Reb, is that you?'

Though startled by her appearance at the foot of the stairs, he managed to restrain himself from going on the offensive and demanding to know what she was doing wandering around in the dark, alone, clad only in a nightdress. The last thing he wanted was to get into another argument with her.

'Yeah… It's me,' he responded inanely, distracted by the tantalising play of moonlight over her features. 'Something wrong?'

'The baby—'

His heart met the soles of his boots, guilt at the way he'd ripped into her earlier tearing at him as he seized her shoulders. 'What's happened? Are you in pain?'

She shook her head, her expression a tad vague before a luminous smile lit her face. 'It kicked! Oh, Reb, our baby kicked!'

The sheer delight in her whisky eyes as she said those words touched him more deeply than anything in his entire life. *Our baby.* Not *my* baby, or *the* baby or *your* baby, but *our* baby. Relief, pride, a thousand emotions he couldn't name rioted within him.

'Well, it wasn't so much a kick as a flutter,' she bubbled excitedly as he caught her wrist and drew her nearer. 'But he's been doing it practically ever since you left.'

He didn't comment on her use of the masculine term.

'Maybe he's angry with me for upsetting his mother, too. God knows he deserves to be.'

She bit her lip, then lowered her head. 'No, I know you were right,' she said softly. 'I didn't consider that other people might need that job more than we did. And I should have known that in Vaughan's Landing especially I wouldn't get hired for any other reason than who I am. In this town people will expect me to stay perched on the pedestal even while they queue up to rock it, hoping I'll topple off.'

As he lifted her chin, his gut cramped at the sight of forlorn resignation in her eyes. 'No one knows better than me what it's like to be pigeon-holed by people,' he said, gently grazing his thumbs over the curve of her cheeks. 'And I shouldn't have done it to you. I'm sorry as all hell for jumping all over you about taking that job. I should've waited to hear your side of things, but...' He sucked in a fortifying breath before making the admission. 'I guess my ego likes the idea of providing for you. Of knowing you need me to take care of you both and—'

'Oooh!' she exclaimed, her eyes widening. Snaring his hands, she gave him a radiant smile as she laid them on the small mound of her belly. 'Wait... He'll do it again in a—'

Even if Amanda-Jayne hadn't felt the next butterfly-soft internal flutter for herself, Reb's awed expression would have identified the moment it happened, for the hard lines of that strong, handsome face softened in a way she'd never have imagined.

'Oh, God.' His words were a whispered prayer. 'I...I felt it.' The ebony eyes he lifted were filled with wonder, but as another embryonic nudge was delivered his delight manifested itself in a joyful laugh. 'Oh, wow! That is so...so...'

She chuckled, the bliss of sharing this moment with him surpassing anything she'd previously experienced. 'So what? Incredible? Amazing? Beautiful?'

'Yeah,' he said huskily. 'As incredible...' his hands

moved slowly outward to caress her hips and then draw her nearer '…as amazing and as beautiful as you are.'

He took her mouth not with the passion she'd come to expect and enjoy, but with a new tenderness that dissolved all trace of the hurt he'd caused earlier. It was a tenderness that prompted both healing and hope. It was a tenderness that caressed not merely her heart, but her soul. The arm around her waist was firm and certain, but the touch of his fingers as they brushed up her neck and across her jaw was as light and hesitant as the first rays of dawn.

Never had Amanda-Jayne felt more treasured.

Never had she felt so happy and yet so close to tears.

Never had she felt so loved…nor wished it were true.

She surrendered to the languid sense of peace that began settling over her mind as his tongue drugged her with the deliciously evocative mixture of mint and tobacco that flavoured this man's kisses. It was a taste she'd rapidly become addicted to and one she knew she'd never have the strength to willingly give up. To compensate her taste buds for his lips moving along her jaw to her ear, her tongue laved the strong corded column of his neck. Her nose brushed against the collar of his jacket, its leather offering a clear contrast to the heat of his skin, and in that instant she decided that if *rightness* had a scent it would be the unique blend of leather, aftershave, soap, grease and the essential maleness of Reb Browne.

And his touch! Dear Lord, his hands wove a magic all of their own. Numerous times she'd been swept away by the transference of their passion, but never had they cherished her as they did now, moving over her with the gentleness of a shadow whilst illuminating her within with the force of a thousand floodlights. How was it that when her heart was racing like a locomotive, when she felt so physically aroused and impatient, she could also feel so mellow and content and more emotionally replete than she'd thought possible?

Then it hit her… *This* was what she'd been seeking that

night when she'd accepted his offer of a drink; what she'd tried to capture as she'd danced in his arms until the early hours of the morning. This aura of inner peace and confidence in her own worth was what she'd been chasing so desperately when she'd willingly accompanied him to his hotel.

The touch of his hands gently massaging her belly forced her eyes open, but she was so mesmerised by his visual caress that it took several seconds to register she was sitting side-saddle across his bike. She had no idea how she'd got there and cared even less to move out of the cradle of his arms.

'You know,' he said huskily, his hands continuing their narcotic caress of her stomach, his lips placing a moist ribbon of kisses along her hairline, 'if you weren't so magnificently pregnant, I'd start this bike, drive flat-chat to an out-of-the-way spot I know next to Saddle Creek…and then I'd make seriously slow love to you until you, me and every one of all those stars up there were burnt out.'

The words, blurring the line between tough guy and poet, sent tingles down her spine.

She smiled up at him. 'Can I take a rain check on that idea?'

'Oh, yeah,' he rasped, once again feasting on her mouth for long, glorious minutes, before carefully sliding her off the bike. Then, in one smooth, sexy movement, which emphasised the rigidity behind the fly of his jeans, he was off the bike and lifting her into his arms.

'I'm too heavy—'

'Shh, you're perfect. The most perfect woman ever created.'

The declaration, murmured against her jugular, sent a tidal wave through her bloodstream. At that moment hearing the statement from Reb was enough to make her believe it.

When they reached their room he sat her on the edge of the bed and immediately began running his fingers through

her hair, over and over. As her entire skeletal system started
to liquefy she couldn't decide if it was the most erotic re-
laxation technique or the most insidious torture. Her head
lolled forward to rest against the solid hardness of his abdomen, and she inhaled hard for another scented fix of
maleness and leather. She was dimly aware of him leaning
toward the bedside table, then within seconds another familiar but not instantly recognisable scent teased her.

Less than a heartbeat later, he was lifting the hem of her
nightshirt, but the recall of what she wore beneath it
prompted her to momentarily resist him.

'I…I'm wearing a really ugly bra,' she warned apolo-
getically.

'You won't be for long.'

The words were no sooner spoken than his deft hands
had discarded the nightdress; the bra went while she was
again being wonderfully distracted by the flavour of his
kiss. It was a distraction she greedily clung to, until the
flattening of his hands against the flesh of her upper thighs
caused her to pull away with a gasp—not because they
were cold, but because they were so *slick*.

'Your oil,' he said, answering her unspoken question as
he guided her back onto the mattress. Still fully clothed, he
knelt on the bed, straddling her calves.

'Y-your…clothes,' she stammered, already fascinated by
his action.

He grinned. 'My clothes are used to exposure to all types
of oils.'

That he'd deliberately misunderstood became a moot
point as she watched him pour more of the herbal concoc-
tion into his palm. The action had her holding her breath
as her sensual curiosity sky-rocketed to somewhere in the
outer stratosphere.

His studiously bent dark head reflected the glow of
moonlight as he liberally applied the perfumed oil along
the outside of her thighs, his touch erotically light in its
repeated roaming from hip to knee and back again. 'What's

it for?' he asked in a voice too tight to be classed as conversational.

'Stretch marks,' she replied, swallowing down her embarrassment. 'And to stop my skin getting itchy and…and dry.'

'It works.' The pads of his fingers continued stimulating her circulation in places far removed from her legs. 'Your skin is like satin.'

His hands roamed to the inside of her thighs, then in one smooth stroke moved to their apex to commence circling there with a promise which sent a wavelet of pleasure rippling through her. When almost immediately his touch returned to her knees, to label her body's reaction as an *anticlimax* was to further torture a brain already having difficulty just keeping her heart and lungs functioning.

He continued to rhythmically repeat the action until in her mind it was a physical chant… *Down…up…around and around… Down…up…around and around and around… Down…up…around and around and around…*

It aroused.

It tempted.

It teased.

It had her clutching at the sheets in both frustration and fantasy. It was simultaneously the most pleasurable experience of her life and the most nerve-racking. He was fully clothed and she needed to touch him. Worse, she needed him to touch more of her. *All of her.*

When she tried to grasp his hands he moved them out of her reach. She uttered an earthy curse of defeat, but it fractured under her uneven breathing and lacked conviction. She was certain this qualified as the most exquisite form of torture ever dealt out to anyone, yet the desire and wealth of emotion in his eyes as he watched her made anger an impossibility. There was *nothing* he could have done physically which could possibly have made her feel more special or appreciated. The problem was, she wanted to *give*, not merely receive.

'Reb…' Her words hardly passed as a whisper. 'Please… It's…it's supposed to go on…on…my stomach and…breasts.'

His grin told her he'd seen through her ruse, but he tripped her heart when his face turned serious and he said, 'I know. I watched you applying it the other morning.'

It was a notion that left her trembling. 'Y-y-you did?'

His hands moved to her hips and he nodded.

'I was in a meeting with a client and had come upstairs to get a sales catalogue I'd forgotten… I was about to call out, then I noticed the bathroom door was ajar. There was steam coming out and then I heard humming…' He paused, his throat revealing an exaggerated swallowing action that a dry-mouthed Amanda-Jayne felt herself mimic.

'A moment later,' he continued, his words thick and huskily delivered, 'I witnessed the most incredibly beautiful and the most physical and spiritually arousing event of my life.' His head came up and his hand moved to caress her throat. Never had his handsome face looked so fiercely intent. 'I was paralysed by poignancy of what I was seeing. Completely and utterly overpowered by the sight. Yet I swear, A.J., not walking in there was the hardest decision I've ever made.

'You were standing gloriously naked, humming a lullaby with one arm cradling our unborn child and the other moving lovingly over your belly… The urge to do it for you…to take that oil and anoint you from head to foot and then make love to you, felt stronger and more instinctive than the need to take my next breath.'

Even before his hand began to simulate her actions of that time, Amanda-Jayne's heart erupted with joy. But when he lowered his head to reverently kiss her stretched, swollen belly it was as if the earth had fallen from its orbit. Tears filled and rolled from her eyes, but as he continued to rain kisses over her body, amid words of praise and adoration, burgeoning happiness and pride made her want to cheer, to laugh…to hope.

Splaying her fingers through his hair, she was torn between the need to explore the images of a future she'd previously refused to allow herself to contemplate and simply seizing the pleasure of this moment for fear it would be gone too quickly. A thousand questions raged for answers in her coherency-depleted brain, but when she finally regathered some measure of composure she asked only one…

'Reb…' she said, her body revelling in the movement of his mouth and her fingers the silky texture of his hair. 'Why…did you stop yourself from coming in?'

The question instantly stilled him. He sighed heavily before answering.

'Because,' he said finally, his head still downcast, 'at that moment I wanted you more…*harder*…and *faster* than ever before. There was a ferocity to my desire, to my need, that made me terrified I might inadvertently harm the baby. *And*,' he said quickly, before she could voice a response, 'and…'

His lengthy pause, stretching beyond what could at best be called uncharacteristic hesitancy, sent a trigger of apprehension through her. Yet something told her not to leave well enough alone.

'And…?' she prompted, despite her misgivings.

He lifted his head and reached gently to cup her cheek. 'And I was afraid that I wouldn't be able to control my lust,' he admitted, 'because God knows it wasn't just a sexual lust that any female could've gratified or I could have dealt with myself… This was an…an *emotional* lust that could only be satisfied by the mother of my child. But I was terrified that the sheer potency—the urgency of what I was feeling—would reduce the whole thing, in your eyes at least, to a wam-bam-thank-you-ma'am exercise.'

Relief had Amanda-Jayne's heart thumping so loud she couldn't hear herself think. Couldn't formulate anything that might come out even remotely coherently. It wasn't a declaration of love—his use of the phrase 'the mother of my child' was fairly generic compared to saying *you*—but the sentiment behind what he'd said, and his reason for doing what he had, had her spirits and her hopes soaring so high they must surely have reached heaven already.

Spontaneous laughter bubbled up out of her, but she pulled his mouth down to hers for a kiss before he could produce more than a hint of a frown.

'I've only got one question,' she said. 'Is the reason you're still dressed some new-fangled braking system you're testing on your libido for fear an eruption of your…er…*emotional lust* might harm the baby?'

The comically sheepish face he pulled gave her the answer.

'Well, in that case…' she grinned '…I suggest you start losing the clothes real fast, or the only person who's going to come to harm is *you*, Reb Browne!' She shoved at his chest. *'When I knock you out and start ripping them off you!'*

'Yes, ma'am!' Wearing a mile-wide grin, he was peeling off his jacket even as he leapt from the bed. 'Anything you say, ma'am!'

'You can cut the "ma'am", stuff,' she said, enjoying his eager strip. 'Because you're got a while to go before we reach the wam-bam part…' She waved the oil bottle. 'You haven't finished the lubrication job you started yet…'

CHAPTER TEN

AMANDA-JAYNE looked back on that night and regarded it as the time her brain had eventually stopped tuning out her heart and she'd finally come to accept that she loved Bad Boy Reb Browne with every ounce of her being, her spirit and her soul. Of course accepting a situation and celebrating it were two entirely different things, since Reb hadn't said he felt the same way.

Oh, he'd indicated that he *liked* her a lot, even cared deeply for her, but the words 'I love you' hadn't been forthcoming. She might have been tempted to believe the concern he showed for her health signified much deeper feelings than mere friendship, had Savvy, Gunna and *especially* Debbie not routinely commented that he'd been equally solicitous of Debbie when she'd been pregnant. The only other way of interpreting his actions towards her was to view them as a deliberate attempt to drive her crazy!

He'd forbidden her to lift anything that weighed more than a tub of butter. Refused to let her drive anywhere unaccompanied. Upbraided her whenever she went up or down the stairs at anything more than geriatric pace and asked her several times a day if she'd taken her vitamins, had her quota of milk and how she was feeling. This morning he'd expressed concern over the fact that she'd locked the bathroom door when she was in there.

'What would happen if you slipped and knocked yourself unconscious in the shower?' he'd asked.

And he hadn't been amused with her glib response of, 'Not a lot, until the water went cold and brought me around again.'

However, the good fortune she felt at just having a caring

husband if not the loving one she craved was enough for her to accept his over-protectiveness with good humour.

'That's a knock-out dress—' Reb's voice was thick with amusement '—but I think you're carrying a bit too much in front these days to fit into it.'

Typically her heart did a jig at the sound of his voice before going into the splits at the sexy picture he made clad in grease-stained clothes, braced against the bedroom doorway. She wasn't sure her intended glare was very credible when she said, 'I could have sworn I mentioned I was becoming particularly sensitive to fat jokes these days.'

'I could've sworn I told you I find you particularly sexy on any day.'

Borrowing a 'Savvyism', she rolled her eyes at him via the mirror, then returned her attention to the ivory sheath she'd been holding against herself before her daydreams about Reb, then the man himself, had distracted her.

'I'm thinking of suggesting to Savvy she wear it for the school formal. It's ankle-length on me, but it'll still look fabulous hitting her at mid-calf. And with her colouring the overall effect will be sensational.' She frowned. 'What do think, Reb? Would she be offended if I offered it to her?'

'Oh, yeah,' he said, coming to stand behind her and wrap his arms around her middle. 'What fifteen-year-old *wouldn't* be offended at having a four-figure designer dress thrust upon her?'

With a blissful sigh, she nestled against him, grateful for even a short reprieve from single-handedly carting around additional weight. How, when just painting her toenails felt like tackling an obstacle course, was she going to survive the next three months?

'It didn't cost anything like that amount,' she assured him, her flash of self-pity vanishing with the soothing motion of his hands across her stomach. 'I modelled it for a charity show and got it for way below retail price.'

He frowned, his attention now solely on the dress. 'You

don't think it's a bit…I don't know…sophisticated for a
kid her age?'

'Well, of course it is! Which is exactly why it should be
perfect for a school dance.'

He looked so adorably perplexed she could do nothing
else but toss the dress on the bed and turn to pull his mouth
down for a kiss.

'Trust me,' she whispered, nibbling his jaw and loving
the feel of his late-afternoon beard against her lips. 'I know
how fifteen-year-old girls think. I used to be one.'

He pulled her closer. 'Yeah, and you hung out with rich
boys in flash cars and drove all us poor guys insane 'cos
we knew we didn't have a chance with you.'

Grinning, she nestled further into his hips. 'Well, you've
got a chance now. There's not a rich boy or a flash car for
as far as I can see.'

'True, but unfortunately there's a '91 Commodore downstairs that needs new sump oil before we close up for the
day.' He grimaced. 'Sorry, babe, but Deb got a call from
the day-care centre that her daughter Alanna's sick—'

'Nothing serious, I hope?'

'Nah!' he said easily. 'Apparently half the school has
that virus that's going around and Alanna's got in on the
act. Anyway, since Deb and Gunna drove to work in only
one car today I let them both go home early. So,' he said,
pausing to steal her breath away with a kiss that scorched
her to the soles of her feet, 'despite the fact I'd rather be
lying under your sexy little chassis unfortunately I'm going
to be stuck in grease up to my elbows and holding the fort
on my own for the next few hours.'

'Ah, poor baby,' she consoled teasingly. 'And you do so
hate having *oil* and grease all over you. Still…' she grinned
'…I'm sure you'll manage to endure it.'

Reb groaned as his body responded with predictable interest. Her words were a deliberately seductive reminder
that what had once been only a therapeutic use of the herbal

lotion for her had developed into a ritualistic sensory treat for both of them.

'Tease,' he muttered, tilting her chin for better access of her mouth. 'I'll endure it just fine with a little sustenance to keep me going.'

As always the taste and feel of her was enough to scatter all thoughts of time and responsibility from Reb's mind. All that mattered to him was that she never failed to return his passion as rapidly as she inspired it.

'It's wonderful how you've managed to teach Leth to pump gas, so he can handle the garage while you two neck.' Savannah's facetious comment succeeded in pulling them apart.

'How come you're home?' Reb asked, finding quiet delight in A.J.'s less than successful attempts not to look fazed by the intrusion. 'I thought you had hockey practice.'

'Netball. But it was called off because the coach is dead or something equally annoying,' she said. 'So where is everyone? The place is deserted downstairs; I could've walked in, raided the till and no one would've been any the wiser.'

'No chance, kiddo,' Reb said easily. 'Old Lethal is pretty possessive of that cash register. However, the mathematics of giving change has him a bit baffled so as soon as you get changed from your uniform I'm going to need you downstairs to help him out.' At Savvy's droll look he added, 'Seriously, kiddo, I need you. I've got a '91 Commodore waiting for me and Gunna and Deb had to go home 'cause Alanna's crook.'

'Great! There goes my lazy afternoon!' Savvy's pained expression switched to wide-eyed curiosity as her eyes drifted to the bed. 'Wow,' she said, darting to pick up the dress. 'This is *gorgeous*.'

'You really think so?' A.J. asked eagerly, crossing to join her.

'Hell, yes.'

Reb smiled at the look of genuine pleasure on his wife's

face, but the quick glance she shot at him clearly said he was going to be superfluous to the ongoing conversation.

'Okay, I'm gone!' he said good-naturedly. 'But, Savvy, you've only got fifteen minutes to do it in.'

The teenager stared blankly. 'To do what in?'

'Try this on,' A.J. responded, shoving the dress at her with a beaming smile. 'If it fits, and you like it, I...I thought you could wear it to the dance.'

Delight and disbelief warred for dominance in the girl's face as she looked from the dress to the older woman. 'You mean it? You'd let *me* wear it?'

A.J. laughed. 'Yes, I mean it, Savvy. As a matter of fact I think you'll look stunning in it.'

'Fourteen minutes!' Reb said with mock gruffness, then, when neither woman paid him the least bit of attention, quietly exited the room, grinning. Just maybe, he thought, heading for the stairs with the flurry of excited female chatter singing in his ears, just maybe they'd started chipping away at yet another domestic hurdle.

Twenty minutes later he decided that the development of a close friendship between his wife and cousin mightn't necessarily make his life quite as perfect as he'd imagined.

'Savannah!' he roared from under the Commodore for the third time. 'Will you *please* get down here? We've got a custom—'

'It's okay, Reb!' A.J.'s voice cut him off. 'Savvy's just popped out for a bit. I'll handle it.'

The sight of the designer-brand sneakers and trim ankles convinced him he wasn't imagining things and rapidly had him propelling himself from under the car.

'A.J.!' he called. 'It's okay. I'll do it.'

'Relax, Reb. I've been here long enough to know how a petrol bowser works,' she said dryly. 'I've even filled my own car a couple times in Sydney where, *stupidly*, most petrol stations are self-serve.'

Reb couldn't help being thrilled that she was obviously prepared to now take an active part in the business, but he did have one concern. 'What about the effect the petrol fumes might have on the baby?'

Shaking her head, she gave him a reassuring smile. 'The baby will be fine. Trust me, I've become mechanically knowledgeable enough to know the pump nozzle goes in the petrol tank, not up my nose.' And, with a wrinkling of that perfectly formed nose, she hurried towards the car Reb knew belonged to the elderly and less than patient Cyril Ferguson.

This, he thought, easing back against the wall to watch the proceedings out of sight of the driver, would be interesting.

Knowing Reb was standing by expecting to have to jump in and help her only made Amanda-Jayne more determined to prove she could do this. So, at the sight of the scowling, bespectacled face of the driver, she widened her smile to idiot-size proportions.

'Good afternoon, sir! How can I help you?'

'Speeding up the service here would be a good start! Where're Reb and his offsider?'

She smiled wider. 'I'm the official…er…offsider today, sir. Gunna's not here and Reb's changing the oil in a spark plug.'

'He's doing *what*?'

The man's facial contortion told her she'd mixed things up.

'Er…I mean a…a…radiator.' Again, it appeared she'd made some error. Either that or the man was in the midst of some sort of seizure. 'That is, he's—'

'Oh, for God's sake, girl, stop your nonsensical babbling and just fill up my tank! And make sure you use *leaded* petrol!' he called, sticking his head out of the window as she moved to the nearest bowser. 'Some fool up in Grafton put that flamin' unleaded, environmental lolly water in it the other day; flamin' car ran like it had whooping cough!'

Grateful he'd spared her making the same mistake, she smiled at his rudeness and swiftly redirected her hand to the bowser marked 'Leaded'. The absence of a tank cap on the driver's side of the car had her tugging the awkward hose around the other...only to stare at the unbroken smoothness of that panel, and she became totally perplexed.

Where the devil was the petrol tank?

Okay, Amanda-Jayne, she thought. You've let the old grouch rattle you. Obviously it *is* on the other side. Calming herself, she trudged back around the rear of the car...and—

'Blast it,' she muttered, walking back to glare at the boot. 'Where the hell do I fill it?' Glancing up, she caught an obviously amused Reb giving her the thumbs-up sign.

Smart-alec! she silently fumed, prepared to sweet-talk the information out of the grumpy old driver before she'd admit to defeat.

Hooking the hose back up, she grabbed the squeegee scraper—*or whatever the stupid thing was called*—and bucket of water and darted to the front of the car.

''Bout time!' the driver grunted. 'How much do I owe you?'

'Oh, nothing yet!' she said cheerfully, sending water in all directions as she attacked the windshield over the man's sputtering protests. 'Gosh, it's lucky you didn't have an accident, driving with all this grime distorting your vision!'

'My vision's fine—'

'And this is such a *gorgeous* old car,' she gushed on. 'I just love the way they tuck all the normally obvious par—' she gasped as her protruding belly and the width of the car bonnet combined to inhibit her ability to reach the centre of the window '...all the normally *obvious* parts out of sight.

'I mean,' she said, pausing in the window-washing to give her muscles a chance to get their second wind, 'don't you think *all* cars should have their petrol caps in the same place as your car?'

When the now confused-looking man didn't immediately pick up his cue to say something helpful like 'No, you idiot! I happen to think having a tank cap concealed *in the roof, above the left-hand-side back passenger door*, is every bit as stupid as you!' she really had no option but to keep digging.

'You know, sir, I'm actually thinking of petitioning the relevant government department and suggesting they pass a law making it compulsory for all future cars to be designed with their petrol caps positioned where it is on this model. Er, tell me... How exactly would you word that request if you were me? That is, how would you describe the *precise* location of the—?'

'Hoy, A.J.!'

The man's shoulder literally sagged with relief when, swivelling his head at the sound of Reb's voice, he spotted him standing outside the workshop.

'Oh! Reb must need my help with something,' she said. 'Excuse me!'

'Anything I can help you with, honey?' he asked, when she reached him. The innocent tone didn't disguise the blatant amusement in his eyes. 'You seem to be having a bit of trouble...er...washing that windscreen.'

'Don't be cute!' she snapped. 'Just tell me where the dumb petrol cap is.'

'It's where it is in all 1982 ZK Ford Fairlanes.'

'Reb!'

He grinned. 'Have I told you today how sexy you look?'

She thumped his arm. 'Yes! Now tell me where the damn petrol tank is!'

'It's behind the rear registration plate,' he said, swinging an arm around her shoulder and starting towards the car.

She stopped dead. *'I'm not going to let you fill that old crank's car,'* she insisted.

'And I'm not going to let you hurt yourself stretching to finish cleaning his windscreen,' he told her. 'So you handle the petrol and I'll tackle the windscreen and cantankerous Cyril. Okay?'

She nodded.

'Oh, and by the way,' she said, raising her voice as they parted so it carried not only to him, but also to the loudly complaining driver, 'I think you're looking particularly sexy today too.' She grinned. 'But then I happen to think you look great covered in oil in or out of bed.'

The car's driver made a choking sound.

Reb's eyes met hers with a promise of retribution.

Her heart told her she'd love every minute of it.

Even before Cyril's refuelled car had pulled onto the road, a Landcruiser drove in. 'I *told* Savvy I needed her here this afternoon,' he said testily, returning the driver's casual salute as he pulled into the far bay.

'Savvy wanted to see Kara and tell her about the dress so I said I'd cover for her. So why don't you go back to whatever you were doing under the car and let me do exactly that?'

Not wanting to dampen her new-found confidence, but having horrifying visions of her filling the obviously brandnew, diesel-only vehicle with regular petrol, he deftly blocked her path to it.

'Nah,' he said, kissing her forehead when her eyes flashed. 'You go ring up the last sale. I'll take care of this one.'

'No, you've got to finish…' A frown of concentration marred her forehead for several seconds. 'Well, finish whatever it was you were doing under that car. I can cope with—'

She broke off as a red Ferrari sped in and came to a sudden stop beside them.

'Hi, guys! Just thought I'd pop round for a nice family visit.' Josh grinned from behind mirrored sunglasses. 'And of course a good home-cooked meal if you absolutely insist.'

A.J. folded her arms and stared pointedly at her brother. 'Honestly, Josh, not everyone has the time to just drop everything and entertain you. As it happens, Reb and I are very busy this afternoon.'

Reb bit the inside of his mouth so hard to keep from laughing at her sudden 'blue-collar work ethic', he nearly drew blood. But he had a hunch the apprentice playboy might turn out to be a godsend.

'Now, honey, I'm sure your brother wouldn't mind working for his supper,' he said quickly. 'Josh, A.J. was just about to serve this customer, so—'

'Amanda-Jayne knows how to pump petrol?' the kid cut in, surprise dripping from his words as he shoved the sunglasses to the top of his head.

'Oh, for heaven's sake, Josh!' his sister chided. 'It's hardly difficult. I only have to ask the driver if they want leaded or unleaded petrol then shove the nozzle in the car, pull it out and take their money.'

Josh's glance cut to the waiting Landcruiser, then knowingly back to Reb's before he said, 'I see... Well, that sounds easy enough, sis. How about I give it a shot with this guy and see how I do?'

'No, Josh—'

'Great idea, Josh!' Reb said over the top of her, opening the Ferrari's door and all but hauling Josh from behind the wheel. 'Let's not keep the customer waiting any longer. Prompt service is repeat business and all that,' he said heartily. 'A.J., you park Josh's car over near the back stairs. That'll give you a chance to get plenty of fresh air before your next exposure to a bout of petrol fumes.'

Two minutes later the Landcruiser was fuelled and on its way as a resigned-looking A.J. made her way back towards Reb and her brother.

'How long do you plan to keep her in the dark about diesel and LPG?' Josh asked out of the side of his mouth.

'I'm not keeping her in the dark. I'm just walking a tightrope between undermining her confidence and confusing her.'

'And I take it you want me to ride shotgun on her in as subtle a way as possible?'

'Exactly,' Reb said. Then added dryly, 'And it'd probably help preserve the business if you could also prevent her from telling any more customers I'm putting oil in radiators.'

When Debbie called that evening to say both she and Gunna had caught their daughter's virus and wouldn't be in for two days, Josh, who was cheerfully digging into a second serving of vegetable lasagne, amazed Amanda-Jayne by immediately announcing he'd be happy to help out for as long as necessary, his private school having already closed for the term break.

But what was even more amazing was that after Deb and Gunna were back on deck Josh still continued to turn up prepared to work each day, and now, after having returned to boarding-school, he arrived on their doorstep *every weekend*. Most recently with a few of his friends.

While Amanda-Jayne loved the idea that her brother felt so comfortable with her and Reb that he sought out their company, one aspect of his visits was bothering her more and more.

'We should have gone to that fête with Savvy and Josh,' she mused aloud, snuggling up to Reb's shoulder one Sunday afternoon.

Turning his attention from the bike race he was watching on TV, Reb gave her a squeeze. 'Nah, I wanted you all to myself. But hey, if you're fed up with being cooped up inside we could go for a drive,' he offered.

She shook her head. 'No. It's okay. I know how much you enjoy watching these lunatics trying to kill themselves by racing in circles at three trillion miles an hour—or some equally stupid speed.'

Reb knew she wasn't any sort of motor racing fan, but she didn't normally sound so morose about it. Killing the picture with the remote, he angled around and tilted her chin towards him. 'Hey, honey what's up?'

'It's just that— Oh, I don't know. Nothing, I suppose.

It's probably just hormonal. These days everything is!' she groused. 'If I get any fatter, I'm going to explode.

'Don't laugh!' she chided. 'The way I look, if went to the beach and lay down to sunbathe, people would probably start throwing water over me and trying to push me into the sea, thinking I'd beached myself.'

Reb began to caress her very noticeable belly. 'Stop being silly. You're barely six months.'

'I know. I'm going to look like *two* whales by the time I get to term.'

'C'mon, A.J.,' he said coaxingly. 'Five months ago I might have expected this sort of self-indulgent, self-pitying act from you, but nowadays it smacks of overkill. So tell me what's really bothering you.'

She sighed, and chewed her bottom lip before answering. 'I'm frightened Savvy's reading more into the interest Josh and his friends are showing in her and Kara than is there.'

'Ah... I see. You think Josh just sees her as a friend and Savvy has more romantic notions.'

'Kinda,' Amanda-Jayne hedged, knowing he didn't see at all, but deciding it would be better for everyone if she didn't disillusion Reb's innocent perception. Besides, this was a typical *girl* problem which she could alert Savvy to with nothing more than a few carefully chosen words.

'You do know he agreed to go to the dance with her?' she said, so Reb wouldn't think she'd abandoned the subject too quickly.

'Mmm. But that's hardly a big deal. They're going in a group with half a dozen others, aren't they?'

'Yes. But don't you think Josh and his private school buddies might be a tad out of place at a V.L. High dance?'

Reb gave a wicked laugh. 'Worried Josh and his sports car-driving cohorts might get on the wrong side of some of the more...er...physical local guys, are you?'

'Among other things, yes,' she said. 'And there's no need to sound so amused by the prospect. That's my brother you're talking about.'

'I know. And Savvy is my cousin.' He winked. 'Trust me, my Bad Boy rep is sufficiently legendary for no one to be stupid enough to cause Savvy, or *any* of her friends, a moment's distress.'

'Oh, gag me with a spoon!' she exclaimed. 'You think you're oh, so tough, don't you, Browne?'

'Yep,' he said smugly, then, with unexpected swiftness, gently tumbled her onto her back on the sofa. 'Wanna try and take me?'

Amanda-Jayne grinned. 'Of course. I make it a rule never to turn my back on a challenge.'

A week later, Amanda-Jayne's 'carefully chosen words' blew up in her face.

'Oh, I get it!' Savvy raged, her hands pulling scathingly at the dress she wore. 'I'm good enough to lend clothes to, but I'm not good enough for your precious brother!'

'Savannah, that's not what I mean at all! You misunderstood.'

'Oh, right! I misunderstood, ''Don't you and your friends go getting too attached to or involved with Joshua and his mates, because, much as I hate to say this, Savvy, I think they're only out for one thing!'''

'Savvy, let me explain—'

'I don't need you to explain! I know precisely what you meant,' the teenager shouted. 'You think that the only possible interest someone from Josh's background could possibly have in someone from mine would be getting laid! Like everyone else in this town, if you're female and live south of the bridge it's automatically assumed you put out on request, on demand and on cue with every guy around!'

'Savvy, stop it right now!' A.J. insisted, grabbing the younger girl's arms. 'It's not *your* morals I'm questioning.'

'Yeah, right! You're implying *your brother's* a slut.'

'No,' she said firmly. 'I'm not. But all those guys are extremely handsome, hormone-driven seventeen- and eighteen-year-olds who have grown up hearing everything you've just accused me of believing. I grew up with boys like them, Savvy. They think responsibility begins and ends with having good manners and carrying a credit card and a condom at all times.

'I'm not saying Josh is like that, Savvy,' she stressed. 'I'm just cautioning you that most guys his age are more interested in adding notches to their belt and scoring with the prettiest girl around than they are in any sort of long-term commitment. Only a fool would look at you and believe you *aren't* going to be the prettiest girl there tonight. I'm not telling you not to be friends with Josh, I'm just cautioning you to be careful.'

Seeing the tears building in the younger girl's eyes, she tempered her tone and slid her hands down to grasp Savvy's.

'Savvy, I love my brother, despite the wedge my step-mother tried to drive between us. But I've come to love you too, which is why I don't want to see you hurt. And it's precisely because Josh *is* my brother and circumstances being what they are that you and he are going to cross paths at family functions a lot in the future. I don't want that to be a painful experience for you, Savannah.'

She gently nudged the girl's chin up. 'Can you understand *now* what I'm trying to tell you?'

Savannah nodded.

'It's crystal-clear to me too, sis!' At Josh's angry voice both women spun in unison to the external stairs. 'But hey, don't count on me at all those family reunions you're planning, 'cos as far as I'm concerned you can go to hell!'

Reb, who'd been tightening the hinges on the bathroom door and had overheard A.J.'s emotive heart-to-heart with his cousin and consequently Josh's unexpected input, emerged to find his pregnant wife standing shellshocked, silent tears streaming down her face as she stared down the outer stairs in her brother's wake. Savvy was also crying, only more loudly and around declarations that she was going to die of embarrassment and would never be able to face Josh again.

'Oh, God!' he muttered, moving to grab his swaying wife before she collapsed.

'Oh, Reb, we've got to go after him! Explain that I didn't mean—'

'Shh, honey, take it easy. You're not going anywhere in this state.'

'Oh, no! What about the dance?' Savvy wailed. 'It starts in an hour and now my make-up is wrecked! Oh, Reb, what am I going to do?'

Reb bit back the curse that rose to his lips and settled a now sobbing A.J. onto the sofa before answering. 'Savannah, if you're going to die of embarrassment, loss of cosmetic face or any other damn thing any time soon kindly do it *quietly*. Because right now all I'm concerned with is calming A.J. down before she brings on labour!'

A.J. snatched at his hands, her face pleading. 'No, no. I'll be all right. Really, Reb…I…will. But please… *please* go find Josh. He's so upset.'

Who wasn't? Reb thought, debating whether he'd placate her more by going rather than staying, as he wanted to.

'Please, Reb, go…hurry.'

'Okay, honey. I'll go, but not until I've phoned Debbie to come sit with you, okay?'

Her face damp with tears, she nodded. 'All right. All right. Just find him for me.'

Reb wondered how long it would be before she calmed down enough to realise that he'd heard enough of her concerns to want to bring Josh and every one of his mates back…dead rather than alive?

Sighing, he reached for the phone. So much for the quiet, romantic evening he'd been planning… 'Hi, Deb, it's me. Listen, we've had a small domestic drama here and I've gotta go find Josh. A.J.'s upset and I don't want to lea— Thanks, Deb; I owe you one.'

CHAPTER ELEVEN

IT TOOK Reb all of five minutes to catch up with Josh, whose car was pulled to the side of the road behind a highway patrol car. Easing back on the throttle, he pulled over in front of the Ferrari, wondering how much worse this night was going to get. He got his answer when he climbed off his bike and recognised the cop standing over Josh's car as the bane of his own teenage life, Constable Richard McCoy.

He'd heard McCoy had been transferred back here, but until now he'd had the good fortune not to run into him. *So much for good fortune!* he thought, pulling off his helmet.

'You okay, Josh?' he asked. *'Josh?'*

The kid thumped the steering wheel. 'Yeah, Reb, I'm just fine!'

'He won't be if he keeps drivin' the way he does. The snooty brat's lucky he came off his ''P'' plates last month or this'd cost him his licence.'

'My night gets any *luckier*,' Josh grumbled, 'I'll get struck by lightning.'

Feeling for the kid, Reb decided to pursue the vain hope that his nemesis had mellowed with age. 'Look, McCoy,' he said. 'Is this *really* necessary? Josh is a clean skin; as far as I know he doesn't have any previous driving offences—'

'I don't!' Josh chimed in earnestly. 'Not even a parking ticket.'

'I imagine you didn't have any priors at one stage too, Browne,' McCoy said, not looking at him. 'But we both know you racked 'em up real quick after the first one.'

For a moment, Reb wondered if the consequences for decking a police officer wouldn't be worth the momentary satisfaction; then he remembered A.J. and knew he wasn't going to let this mongrel shadow his future as he had his past. But watching the guy begin to inspect the car in the hope of nailing Josh for something in addition to speeding made the *déjà vu* of the moment too strong to keep him mute.

'Get real, Constable McCoy,' he said, knowing Josh paid more attention to the condition of his tyres than A.J. ever would. 'You seriously think you'll be able to find a reason to slap a defect sticker on a car registered to a *Vaughan*?

'Look, we both know the law allows for cautions; can't you just give the kid one and forget the whole incident?'

'I don't believe in cautions, Browne. *You* oughta remember that,' he sneered. 'And I don't care what his name is; I'm charging him.'

'For what? Being eighteen and upset?'

'For doin' a hundred and fifteen in a one ten zone.'

Reb shook his head. 'You know, McCoy, for someone who rumour has it was busted down a few ranks and booted back to Vaughan's Landing because of an attitude complaint from a citizen, it seems to me you're not exactly taking the right steps to address your PR problem.'

The man's eyes narrowed. 'Don't push me, Browne. If I'd had the radar gun on you comin' outta that curve I'd be writin' you up right now too.'

Reb smiled. 'Then I guess it's my lucky night, not yours, eh?'

With a hateful glare, the cop ripped off the ticket and tossed it along with Josh's licence back into his lap. 'You *both* got lucky tonight,' the cop added, slowly closing his ticket pad. 'I saw the way you came round that curve, Browne; whatever *minor* success you might've enjoyed on the Grand Prix circuit, just remember you're back on my turf now. I'm going to be watching you like a hawk.'

'I appreciate the tip, McCoy,' Reb said smoothly. 'Oh,

and by the way, *thanks*… If it hadn't been for the burning desire you instilled in me to leave this town, I wouldn't have ever made it onto the pro circuit. Those *minor* successes were enough to change my life for the better!'

The cop spun on his heel and strode towards his car. Reb watched him go, waiting to see if he'd throw his foot out and knock the stand from under his bike as he'd once done years ago. He didn't. In fact he all but jogged to get into his car and away.

'I take it you and him have a past,' Josh said.

Reb turned to look at him. 'Yeah. And one day I might tell you all about it, but right now we've got other things to talk about.' With that he walked around and climbed into the passenger seat.

'Okay,' he said on a resigned sigh. 'How much did you overhear, Josh?'

'More than I wanted to.'

'I heard the whole lot.'

The kid paled ten shades. 'Oh, great! So now you believe that I'm only hanging around to score with Savvy and you're going to start throwing punches left, right and centre to teach me a lesson! Fine!' he said, turning to face Reb and tapping his chin. 'Go for it! What do I care? My own sister thinks I'm scum, you might as well!'

'Take it easy, Josh; I'm not here to teach you a lesson.' Reb stifled a grin at the kid's sceptical expression. 'Although for the record,' he added, 'if I *were*, trust me…it would take only one punch.

'Furthermore your sister doesn't think you're a scumbag; *she loves you*. The only reason I'm here instead of being back home, where she's sobbing her heart out over what happened, is because she wants the chance to try and explain things to you.'

'What's to explain? I heard what she said.'

'Yeah, but you haven't analysed the situation any better than she has.'

'Analysed what situation?'

'Well, for starters, A.J.'s physical state and the havoc it's playing with her hormones, not to mention her emotions.'

Reb sighed. Josh's expression let him know he wasn't getting off to a roaring start in trying to explain the situation. Patting himself down in search of his cigarettes, he came up empty, then remembered he'd stopped carrying them three days ago.

'You got a smoke, Josh?'

'A.J. doesn't approve of smoking.'

'I know,' Reb said, digging into his pockets for a stick of the gum he was certain was going to give him RSI of the jaw. 'Which is why I'm driving myself insane trying to quit. You don't seriously think I'm putting myself through this for the sake of my health, do you?' he quipped, opening the console ashtray to dispose of the gum wrapper and finding several white-tipped, lipstick-stained butts lying in the bottom.

'Ah, Savvy's preferred brand,' Reb observed, sending a sideways glance to Josh. 'Hope you're not encouraging her in vices I'm trying to break both of us from.'

'No! Gee, why is everyone suddenly convinced I'm trying to corrupt Savvy's morals, health and every other damned thing? I *like* her; I think she's a great kid, but—'

'Okay, okay! I get the picture.'

'No, I'm not sure you do!' he spat back. 'I'll admit I'm not a saint, but, contrary to what Amanda-Jayne thinks, I don't exist for the sole reason of laying every girl I meet! Has it occurred to anyone that maybe Savvy *isn't* the only reason that I like hanging out at the garage? And—'

'It's occurred to me.'

Josh went silent, his expression one of disbelief.

'It's true, Josh.'

'Yeah, right.'

'Look, I know from personal experience that trust isn't a commodity that's all that easy to give when a person hasn't had much experience at receiving it, but at least hear me out before you decide I'm lying.'

The younger man hesitated a moment before saying, 'Well, get on with it.'

That the kid was prepared to listen only solved half of Reb's problem…he didn't have a clue where to go next. In the end he decided he'd just have to fly blind.

'Righto,' he said firmly, hoping to at least sound as if one of them knew what he was saying. 'For starters you've got to understand that it's not easy getting used to being part of a real family when you've never had one. Or trying to be a parent when you've had no one to take your example from.'

'You're talking about Amanda-Jayne.'

'I'm talking about *all* of us. You, me, Savvy and, yeah, A.J. But we'll start with her 'cos she's the catalyst of all this.'

Reb took a moment to formulate everything he wanted to say into some sort of order, anxious to sort things out as quickly as possible so he could get back and make sure A.J. was all right.

'To begin with, Josh,' he said finally, 'for all the wealth and social advantages you and A.J. had growing up, your family was every bit as dysfunctional as mine and Savvy's and it's no secret what that was like. On the surface the Vaughan existence looked ideal, but scratch that surface and we both know what it was really like, don't we, Josh?'

At the sad, uncomfortable expression on the kid's face he answered the question himself.

'Your old man spent more time building the family business than he ever did building a family. My take on things is that to him his kids were merely walking billboard advertisements for the Vaughan name and its wealth. Your mother pretty much agreed, but she resented A.J. so much, she made a career out of making her life difficult at every opportunity. You, on the other hand, she pampered and showered with every material thing you could possibly ever desire, *except*,' he said, pointedly, 'love and affection aren't material things.'

'I survived. I never asked for pity.'

'No, and neither did A.J. or Savvy or me. In different ways each of us toughed it out. We all went on thinking we were independent and strong individuals who could survive on our own, until suddenly something happened to make our worlds collide.'

'You and Amanda-Jayne got married.'

Reb didn't bother to say that wasn't *precisely* the collision point, grateful that the kid was at least listening and following him.

'Our marriage was a giant culture shock for A.J. and the start of a huge learning curve for her, Savvy and me. You came to the wedding, but then faded back into your own world while the rest of us butted heads and scraped our emotional knees and elbows trying to get a handle on this whole family concept.'

He smiled. 'Then I guess all those maternal instincts of A.J.'s began to kick in and somehow she got things to start blending. I'm not saying it was easy for her or us, but things just started to…to *click*. Savvy stopped being so surly and rebellious. She stopped sneaking out at night and started spending more time at home. Even her grades picked up.

'As for me…' Reb paused to try and condense all the positive changes that had occurred in his life these few short months. Lord, the list was endless! 'Well, mostly I guess I lost that big chip I've carried on my shoulders all my life.' He grinned. 'Well, a considerable chunk of it anyway. I still *wanted* to deck that copper McCoy something fierce, but I didn't. What stopped me was the changes A.J.'s brought into my life; because of her I now want to focus on my *future*, not my past.'

He slunk lower in the seat, angling himself so he could look directly at Josh. 'Now let's talk about you. One day, after not having so much as phoned since the wedding, you turn up out of the blue at the garage. I figure that with it being the school break and your mother still sulking over in Europe you were at a loose end and decided to amuse yourself by checking out how your socialite sister was coping with life on the wrong side of the tracks... How am I doing with my take on things so far?'

Josh shrugged, looking uneasy. 'Just go on.'

'Okay, then... Well, you turn up at the garage and find not only is your once prissy sister pumping gas, but yourself commandeered into action too. You've got a strong enough interest in cars not to be bored and you've got nothing better to do, so you think, What the hell? One day won't kill me.

'Surprisingly, though, you find yourself having fun. You enjoy the hit-and-miss informality of the dinner we shared that night and so you offer to back up for another day of the same... You keep backing up, even sleeping on our sofa, until even Savvy and all her friends start accepting you for just being Josh, A.J.'s kid brother, as opposed to Joshua Vaughan, the kid who's got everything they haven't.

'Then suddenly the vacation ends and you're back in that swank boarding-school of yours and you should be happy, but damn! You're missing that sofa! You're missing the inane jokes we toss around over the best lasagne this side of Italy. So you start coming back to Vaughan's Landing *every* weekend and even bring friends with you. But not to spend time lazing around the Olympic-size pool at your ancestral home or stirring up the locals by cruising town with a carload of your wealthy mates... No, you come home to pump gas, hang out with kids from the local high school and sleep on a sofa.

'You come home,' Reb repeated. 'Because for the first time in eighteen years you feel like you've got a *family* who cares about you to come home to.'

Josh raked his fingers through hair Reb figured had missed at least two of his usual three-figure haircuts. 'A family who cares about you doesn't say what A.J. did.'

'Everyone makes mistakes, mate. A.J.'s only one is that, having realised the value of the family bond that's grown between the four of us, she's desperate to hang onto it. But she's scared that if Savvy's crush on you gets out of hand then things will start falling apart in the future. So those novice-level, newly developed maternal instincts of hers took over and she jumped in and tried to avert that happening.' He paused to give the kid an assessing look.

'She loves you, Josh, but she's grown to love Savvy too. She doesn't want *either* of you to be hurt, but right now she sees Savvy as being the more naive and vulnerable.

'Facts, Josh… Something like eighty-five per cent of girls from this part of town are pregnant before their eighteenth birthday! Six girls out of Savvy's grade at school this year are already pregnant and one, *at fifteen*, has a toddler!'

'Fact, Reb!' he shot back. 'I'm not responsible!'

The comment caught him off guard.

'You and A.J. might've got caught out, but I haven't. What's more, I'm not such a lust-crazed idiot that I go after *gaol-bait*.'

Reb knew grown men who wouldn't have had the guts to call him on that and surprisingly, instead of anger, he felt admiration for Josh. *Damn, he really liked this kid!* Now all he had to do was work out a way to keep Savvy fifteen for the rest of her life, because, while Josh might be feeling as brotherly as all get out *now*, he'd bet his favourite bike his cousin wasn't going accept the situation indefinitely. A.J. might have overreacted tonight, but Reb hadn't been entirely blind to his young cousin's fascination for Josh. Now, however, wasn't the time to get bogged back down in that.

'Okay, message received,' Reb said. 'You like Savvy, but on a purely Platonic basis.'

'*Exactly!* And I'd appreciate you passing it on to both her and your wife.'

'*My wife*,' Reb said, 'needs to hear it from her *brother*. More importantly she needs to know that he loves her every bit as much as she loves him.'

Josh's head dipped under Reb's insistent stare. 'I…I…need time to calm down before I talk to her.'

'No, A.J. is the one who needs calming down. She's pregnant, Josh, and believe me I'm not going to have her upset for one second longer than necessary. Therefore what you need to do and what you're going to do is to start this car and follow me back to the garage.' Reb made sure his tone left no room for argument.

Josh looked at him for a moment then sucked in a resigned breath and nodded. 'Fair enough… I'll be right behind you.'

Overwhelmed with relief, Reb slapped the younger man's shoulder in silent gratitude before slipping out of the low-slung car.

'Hey, Reb,' Josh called before he'd taken two steps to his bike. 'Thanks. For what it's worth, I'm real glad my sister finally found someone to love her as much as you do.'

The kid's words slammed into him with such cyclonic force, Reb marvelled that he was still standing. He marvelled also at how he'd managed to survive so long when he was the world's all-time idiot. *Emotional lust! Aw, hell! How stupid could a guy get?* He didn't *emotionally lust* after A.J., he was *in love* with her. And had been for…well, only God knew how long because *he* sure hadn't had the brains to recognise it.

He jumped as the Ferrari's horn blasted.

'Hey, I thought you wanted me to follow you home, Reb?' Josh frowned. 'What are you waiting for?'

What was he waiting for? Only to hear the most precious person in his life tell him what no one else ever had…*that she loved him*.

Three days later Amanda-Jayne decided she was probably never going to find out what had transpired between Reb and her brother on the night of the dance and that she should just be satisfied that Josh had returned to the apartment and given her the chance to repair the damage she'd inadvertently done. When she'd quizzed Reb as to what he'd said to Josh he'd simply shrugged and said it was 'guy stuff'. Her brother had been equally vague; however, that was probably because he'd bought the story Debbie had concocted for a highly embarrassed Savannah that the *only* reason she'd asked Josh to come to the dance in the first place was to make another boy jealous. Josh's expression had revealed he wasn't sure whether he should be relieved or insulted.

Amanda-Jayne smiled, conceding that despite her rough edges Debbie's mind was every bit as elegantly devious as any debutante's. She also felt that a huge chunk of the animosity which had existed between herself and the other woman had been eroded that night, when Debbie had willingly shared her experience of childbirth with her and offered advice on enduring it.

Yet, while the explosive events of that night had put her relationships with her brother, Savvy and Debbie on a more stable footing, it bothered her how tense and uneasy Reb had been since then. There wasn't one particular incident that she could single out as evidence of this, until late one Tuesday when a well dressed, fifty-ish man breezed into the garage, just as she and Reb were locking up for the day.

'Jack!' Reb exclaimed, alarm momentarily flashing across his features. *'What the devil are you doing here?'*

The man laughed. 'Hello to you too, mate.'

Reb's tension was evident in his slow response to the man's proffered handshake and the way his gaze kept skating past Amanda-Jayne. He was definitely uncomfortable. She couldn't guess why, but instinct told her this wasn't one of the myriad of salesmen who regularly came in to peddle mechanical parts. A good clue was that none of them wore genuine Rolexes and instantly she too began to feel nervous. When the man's smile drifted to her she returned it with a polite, cautious one of her own. Then Reb made a very perfunctory introduction.

'Er, Jack, this is Amanda-Jayne. A.J., Jack Edgemen. So tell me, Jack,' he hurried on, pre-empting any further exchange between the two of them, 'what are you doing here?'

'I'm on my way back from inspecting the Queensland operation and want to discuss that expansion idea with you.'

'Oh. Right. Sure. Everyone's gone for the day so we won't be interrupted. Er, come through to the office,' he said, then turned to Amanda-Jayne. 'We'll probably be discussing business for a while, honey, so tell Savvy I'll feed Lethal before I come up.'

Reb's smile and the endearment might have made it look like a pleasant request, but his tone had 'Dismissed!' threaded right through it. It would have been gratifying to snap back with, Tell her yourself! but she bit her tongue, forced a smile and nodded to Jack Edgemen, who was observing everything with rude interest.

'Nice to meet you, Mr Edgemen.'

'Er, you too, Amanda-Jayne...*such as it was.*'

Pretending not to notice the irritated look Reb shot at the man, she walked from the office as serenely as her ballooning size and temper would allow. *Something was definitely going on!* And if Reb couldn't trust her enough to share his problems with her voluntarily...well, then, she'd just have to resort to deviousness to discover what they were. She didn't feel a bit guilty about this because turnabout was fair play and at least she wasn't going to stick a private investigator on *him*!

'I can't believe,' Jack said twenty minutes later, 'that you've suddenly gone cold on this idea, Reb. *You* were the one trying to talk *me* into investing in something like this a few months back.'

Reb could have corrected him and said that the last time

he'd pushed for them to expand into the South Australian motorcycle market had been exactly *seven* months ago, on the nineteenth of October. For it had been after Jack had left the bar where they'd met for drinks to discuss the project that he'd run into A.J. Now it wasn't so much the case that he'd had a change of mind on the concept as he'd had a change in his life.

'I know, Jack,' he said, his tone apologetic. 'And for what it's worth I still think it's an incredible investment opportunity, but the timing of it isn't right for me now. I'm not in a position to commit to the project. The baby's due in a couple of months and, well, to be truthful things are going better for me now than I dared hope. I'm not prepared to gamble what I've got now.'

'Reb, look... I can understand that you don't *personally* want to tie yourself to an interstate project under the circumstances, but I'm willing to take on all that stuff,' Jack pressed.

'I appreciate that, mate, but I wouldn't feel right just coming along for a free ride and, like I said, I can't see my way clear right now to make that sort of business commitment. Maybe down the track a bit...'

Jack Edgemen sighed. 'Okay, okay. But I'd like to go ahead with things anyway, so as a favour to me would you at least come to Sydney and meet with the other investors? If there are any holes in the proposal you're more likely to spot them than I am.'

Glad to do something that didn't leave him feeling as if he'd completely bailed out on his friend, Reb nodded. 'When?'

'The sooner the better as far as I'm concerned. What suits you?'

'Well, I'll be in Sydney Thursday; Amanda-Jayne's got a specialist's appointment. Any chance you could set something up that fast?'

'No worries. These guys are keen with a capital K.' He

pulled a face. 'At least they were when they thought you'd be coming in on the deal.'

'They'll stay keen, Jack. A project like this should bring you some real nice returns.'

'But not enough to sway you, huh?'

Reb grinned. 'Nope. I've got too much invested in my personal life at the moment to handle the excitement of a business gamble right now.'

That night, before Reb had a chance to tell A.J. he had a business meeting before her specialist's appointment and suggest she meet a friend while he attended it, she announced that Savannah would be accompanying them to Sydney.

'But that's a school day,' he protested.

'Apparently the teaching staff are having some sort of Education Department training day. The kids have the day off, so I invited Savvy to come to Sydney with us. It'll be perfect.' She smiled. 'You don't like me driving by myself so this means Savvy and I can go shopping or something while you're at your meeting.'

While she was obviously pleased with her idea, Reb was less than thrilled. After Jack had left he'd decided the long trip south would provide a perfect opportunity to come clean with A.J. and tell her *everything* about himself—a perfect opportunity if only because, stuck within a moving vehicle, she wouldn't be able to storm off before he could explain all the reasons he'd been less than honest with her. Having Savvy along butchered his plans for a personal discussion.

To make matters worse, on the morning of the trip A.J. stubbornly insisted they make it in her car rather than his four-wheel drive. No amount of reasoning from him, nor complaints from Savvy that she'd be cramped past breathing point in the small rear seat of the convertible, could get her to change her mind or her argument that she wouldn't be comfortable negotiating city traffic between one shopping mall and the next in the larger vehicle. Reb, who'd weeks ago given up trying to identify at what stage of pregnancy a woman went from being difficult to reason with to being impossible to reason with, in the end decided it was easier and more expedient to simply give in to her.

Amanda-Jayne decided that the trip to Sydney had never taken so long. By the time Reb steered the car into a parking area outside a large motorcycle showroom, she was ready to shove him out from behind the wheel. As interested as she was in hearing about how this was where he'd worked when he'd first come to Sydney twelve years ago, she didn't want to hear it *now*! She was far more concerned with the fact that she had less than twenty-five minutes to navigate her way through heavy Sydney traffic to make her appointment on time.

No longer able to comfortably slide from the passenger to the driver's seat, she darted out of the door, around the car and was behind the steering wheel turning over the engine before Savvy had removed herself from the back seat. 'C'mon, Savvy, hurry it up,' she urged.

'What's your rush?' Reb asked, watching her with amusement. 'Afraid the shops will sell out before you get there?'

With her foot hovering over the accelerator she dutifully accepted his kiss on the cheek as her mind catalogued how much she had to get done and how little time she had to do it.

'You definitely think your meeting will only go on until about two, right?' she asked anxiously.

'*Yes*, A.J. Stop worrying,' he said, giving her another patient smile. 'I promise we'll make it to Dr Geermaine's offices by four-thirty. You won't be late for your appointment.'

Unable to tell him that she'd switched the appointment to next week so that wasn't what was worrying her, she smiled and nodded at his suggestion that they have fun.

Then, releasing the parking brake, she accelerated towards the exit…and with luck the future she'd always dreamed of.

'Er, A.J.…?' Savvy said fifteen minutes later as she zipped lanes to escape a crawling truck in front of her. 'That's the second major shopping mall you've driven past. *Exactly where* are you planning on shopping?'

She laughed, shooting her passenger a quick look. 'Oh, I'm not going shopping, Savannah…I'm going *selling*. But hopefully I'll manage to buy a happy future at the same time!'

Impatient with the drone of the man trying to convince him to reconsider his refusal to invest money into a prototype for an Australian-designed and manufactured motorcycle, Reb glanced out of the window of Jack's office in time to see A.J. and a worried-looking Savvy emerging from a taxi. Disbelief had him doing a double-take. Then, with fear running a relay around his nervous system, he bounded out of his chair and raced from the room at a speed which had him arriving at the entrance of the showroom the same time the two women did.

After checking and seeing no visible signs of injury, he carefully pulled A.J. into his arms. 'Thank God you're okay!' He pulled back. *'You are okay, aren't you?'*

'I'm fine, Reb, I—'

'Oh, thank God!' Holding her close, he fought to regulate his heartbeat before directing his next question at his cousin. 'What about you, Savvy? You okay?'

She gave a nervous laugh and shrugged. 'I think I'm in shock.'

He nodded. 'Okay, what happened?'

'I'm not sure you want to know,' Savvy said dryly. 'Which is why I'm making myself scarce.'

'Oh, no, you're not!' he said, when she tried to move past him. 'I want to know how the accident happened.'

The woman in his arms struggled to free herself. 'Oh,

Reb!' Her smile was sympathetic. 'We didn't have an accident.'

'You didn't?' He blinked. 'Then where's the car? Why were you getting out of a taxi?'

'Because—' A.J. started.

'I'm outta here!' Savvy said, her words and action unified.

'Because,' A.J. repeated, her voice not entirely steady, 'I *sold* the car.'

'You did what?'

Even when she repeated the words, digging frantically through her shoulder bag, Reb couldn't mentally reconcile them.

'But *why*? A.J., you love that car.'

Smiling, she thrust a thick manila envelope into his hands. 'Not as much as I love you.'

His heart melted. His lungs froze. With emotion blurring his vision and thickening his throat he was incapable of doing anything, bar staring at the woman in front of him. With those whisky-brown eyes gazing up at him, full of warmth, his brain was scarcely aware of Jack hovering only metres away asking if everything was all right.

'Everything's fine, Mr Edgemen. Reb will be right in,' A.J. responded, her gaze darting over his shoulder, before returning to his.

'I'm not sure,' she whispered, 'exactly how much you need to get in on this deal with Jack, but what's in here…' she tapped the envelope he'd forgotten he held '…should be enough to get you started. We can figure out a way to get the rest later. Now quick,' she urged, giving him a subtle shove. 'Get back in there and—'

'You sold the car because you thought I needed money.'

She blushed. 'I…er…*overheard* you telling Jack the other night that you thought the idea was an incredible investment opportunity, but that you weren't in a position to commit to it. Because of…well, because of the baby and me—'

'A.J., I—'

'Shh,' she said, placing a finger across his lips. 'There was real excitement in your voice when you were talking to Jack and I don't want you to miss this opportunity. The car isn't and never has been as important to me as you've become, Reb Browne,' she told him in a tone that wrongly implied she'd told him this countless times before. 'And it's silly that you should have to forfeit a fabulous business opportunity when I'm driving around in a totally impractical car!' She winked. 'Besides, a baby capsule is going to look ridiculous in a convertible. So you just get back into that meeting and tell those investors you want *in*. Okay?'

'You really mean that?'

'Of course I do! Reb, if you think this is a good deal—'

'Not that! I mean do you really love me?'

The sparkle in her eyes softened to a gentle glow a nanosecond before she nodded. 'I love you more than I could ever tell you, Reb Browne.'

Feeling as if his heart had just inflated to the size of the Earth, Reb pulled her fiercely against him. 'Oh, honey, I've been *dying* waiting to hear you say that. But you couldn't have shown me your love better than you've just done.'

Though Amanda-Jayne wished he'd have verbalised his own love immediately, a part of her heart told her to be patient; that later, when they had no audience, Reb would be more than eloquent in revealing his feelings. It was, however, difficult not to cling to him when he gently eased her from him.

'Jack,' he said, looking not at the man behind him, but deeply into her eyes, 'my wife thinks this deal is too good to turn down, so I guess you better get back in there and tell them I'm in.'

'Great! But you can tell them yourself.'

'Sorry, Jack. Right now I've got a few things I need to tell my wife.' Lowering his head, he took her mouth in a short soft kiss. 'Like the fact that I'm crazy about her,' he whispered so only she could hear. 'That picking her up in a bar was the smartest move I ever made… That I'm prouder than hell that she's going to be the mother of my child… And that I love her more than life itself.'

The hefty kick that nudged his stomach indicated that the words seemed to surprise not only A.J. but also their child. Automatically his hand moved down to soothe it.

'Y-y-you *love* me?' she asked, her voice tight, her eyes swimming with tears. 'Really?'

'Oh, yeah.'

She threw herself against him, her hands and lips feverishly moving over him. 'Oh, Reb! I can't believe it! I love you so much! I *need* you so much! Reb…'

Struggling to contain his own joy and disbelief amid her gleeful, sobbing declarations of love, Reb held onto her as tightly as he could. No one had ever told him they loved him. No one… Except this amazing, beautiful woman who'd managed to fulfil not only his fantasies, but also dreams he'd never dared to have. Amanda-Jayne Vaughan loved *him*. Bad Boy Reb Browne had somehow won the heart of the princess.

As incredible as the idea still seemed to his brain, his heart recognised it as the truth—just as his heart knew she'd forgive him his deception about his true financial situation. All that was left to do now was to tell her about it.

CHAPTER TWELVE

FOR a long time Amanda-Jayne simply stared at the huge single-storey Federation-style home, coming to terms with what she'd learned. Bad Boy Reb Browne wasn't merely a struggling mechanic who'd stretched himself to his financial limit when he'd paid off all her bills; he was a former professional motorbike racer who'd earned sufficient money on the circuit to invest in his former sponsor's, Jack Edgemen's, chain of motorcycle dealerships. Along the way the dealership had grown to be the second largest in the country and the investment he'd been discussing with Jack today was seen as the way to push it to number one.

Conscious of the concerned gaze Reb fixed on her and the tension radiating from him, despite the way he appeared to lean casually against the bonnet of Jack's Edgemen's Jaguar, Amanda-Jayne didn't know whether she wanted to laugh, cry or punch him out. This might not have been on the scale of Vaughan House but, situated in a semi-rural area on Sydney's north-western outskirts, which boasted the hideaways of an increasing number of artists and professionals, it was light-years away from the garage apartment.

'You really own...' she spread her arms to encompass the manicured lawns, which he'd said were 'roughly four acres', the house and a huge brick building that to her mind didn't look sufficiently well ventilated to be a horse stable '...all of this?' He nodded. 'And what's that used for?' she asked, still curious about the brick building.

'When I had the place built I intended it to be a garage where I could muck around with my bikes. I think the last

177

tenants who were here used it as some sort of glorified games room for their kids.'

She turned to give him an accusing look. 'All this time, I've been worrying myself sick that I was adding to the financial strain of keeping the garage afloat. I only applied for that job because you'd acted like the price of that dress Savvy wanted was beyond you.'

'It wasn't the cost but the dress itself I had reservations about. I swear, A.J.,' he said earnestly, 'I wasn't trying to deliberately mislead you about that. Or the ring.'

'Just everything else, huh?'

Reb knew he deserved her disdain, but there was none of it in her smile as she walked towards him with her arms around their unborn child. But she stopped about a metre away.

'I take it since no one let anything slip to me that Savvy and everyone else at the garage was in on the poverty conspiracy too?'

'No. That was just dumb luck.'

'And that photograph on the bedroom wall is of you, isn't it?'

He nodded. 'It was taken at Philip Island in my first year of racing in the 500cc championship. It's special to me because it was my only major race in Australia. I did a few years in the 250 class, then moved on to Superbikes and then back to the Grand Prix scene and racing 500s. I crashed out midway through my second season on GP 500s and then my uncle died and I had Savvy to look after so that was that.' He shrugged. 'I picked up my life in Vaughan's Landing.'

'Do you miss it—the racing?'

'I did until you came into my life,' he admitted honestly. 'Now I don't ever want to do anything that might take me away from you or our baby.'

'Good!' she said firmly. 'Because I absolutely hate the thought of you doing something that dangerous. Were you ever badly hurt?'

He grinned. 'Let me put it this way…if the baby is born with metal pins in its wrist and knee he or she will have inherited them from me.'

She pulled a face, then turned once more to study the house. 'Reb, why buy a property and build a house like this and then not live in it?'

He sighed. 'Because I'd always promised myself that one day I'd own a real home, on a par with those you see in magazines… Trouble was, I couldn't bring myself to live in it. I couldn't get past the crazy idea that I was selling out to what and who I really was. I felt like I'd let the remarks of all the people who said I'd never amount to anything have too much influence.'

She spun back to him. 'Oh, Reb, that's silly,' she said gently. 'You proved them wrong; if anything you should have shoved their noses in it.'

He pulled a wry face. 'I suppose…but when you've spent a lifetime craving to be accepted for yourself, being accepted for how much cash you've got doesn't seem like such a victory.'

'You're right,' she said. 'It isn't. But we've both ended up victorious, haven't we?'

He nodded, smiling. 'We have if you can forgive the fact that I've got more money than you expected.'

'I'll *try* and not see your wealth as a hardship,' she teased, then her expression became uncertain again. 'You have to also forgive me for being less than honest with you…' She took a deep breath. 'I've already explained about how I paid off the car, but the rest of the story is that I never really intended to marry you. What I mean is that right up until I said "I do" I was counting on Patricia releasing my allowance so I wouldn't have to go through with it,' she admitted, studying her shoes.

'Gosh darn!' Reb said dryly. 'That thought never crossed my mind.'

Her head jerked up. 'You mean you *knew*?'

'Not really, but, honey, *no one* was more surprised than

I was when you were still standing beside me at the end of the ceremony.'

'Wanna bet?' she laughed.

'Nope,' Reb said. 'I want you to come here so I can kiss you and show you how grateful I'm always going to be to your stepmother.'

Her compliance was swift and earnest and their kisses sprinkled with endearments which suddenly had more depth, meaning and power than ever before. The subtle but elemental difference of knowing her love was returned touched Amanda-Jayne in a way she couldn't describe, but Reb, obviously sensing it too, managed to put it into words.

'We're not the Bad Boy and the Perfect Princess any more,' he said, grazing his thumbs along her cheeks. 'We've outgrown Vaughan's Landing and its image of us. So, I've been thinking… Maybe it's time to get the dust of the place off our boots for good. What would you say if I suggested we move here for a while and see what it's like to be *normal*? To live in a place where no one knows us?'

Electric excitement raced through her. 'You're serious? You mean we could move…*here*?'

'Any place you like, honey.'

'Oh, Reb,' she yelped excitedly, throwing herself into his arms. 'I love you so much! I never thought I could be this happy. That *anyone* could be this happy!'

'I know,' he murmured. 'But what's more amazing is that you loved me even when you thought I was just a lousy mechanic.'

She pulled back before their lips met and grinned at him. 'True, but I wanted your baby even when I thought you were nothing more than the town Bad Boy.'

He caught her chin. 'Good,' he said darkly. ''Cos I can't promise that from time to time I won't regress.'

She threaded her fingers into his hair and drew his face nearer. 'I hope you do…'cos I've discovered I like being *bad* with you.'

*   *   *

For Amanda-Jayne the next six weeks passed in a flurry of moving, house-furnishing, nursery decoration and the irritation of waking several times every night to hurriedly waddle to the bathroom only to find she didn't have to go when she got there. Reb, however, was a master at finding delicious ways to compensate her for being dragged from a restful sleep by their over-active child. However, two weeks before her due date, when she awoke to find herself lying in a very wet bed, Amanda-Jayne's first reaction was to burst into tears of self-disgust... The second was to scream as a knifing pain cut low in her abdomen.

Forty minutes later she was breathing as hard as she could on some sort of mask which was making her light-headed, but not numbing the pain to any noticeable extent.

Three hours later she was swearing at Reb, Savvy and the *oh, so pleasant* nurses and telling them that childbirth was just too hard and she'd happily stay fat and pregnant for ever and *never* complain about it if they'd let her go home. *Now.*

Ten hours after that, she was still a tad light-headed, but this time with joy as she sat propped up, proudly cradling her nine-pound-four-ounce son who'd eventually been delivered by an emergency Caesarean. Curiously, there was no sign of the motorbike Amanda-Jayne had insisted he must have been straddling during her futile efforts to deliver him naturally. Nevertheless, for all the difficulties of her labour, she was convinced that Travis Joshua Browne was *the* most beautiful child ever born. And the most wonderful husband in the world agreed with her. So too did Savannah and Josh, although the latter was still pushing for his nephew's names to be reversed.

When the nurse came and insisted for the third time that Travis be returned to the nursery, Amanda-Jayne felt as if they were taking away a part of her and demanded a wheelchair so she could accompany him. The request was declined on medical grounds, so she dispatched Reb, Savvy and Josh to ensure Travis came to no harm on the journey.

She then fretted until Reb returned, alone, to report their son was in good hands and, under the adoring eyes of his uncle and cousin, was sleeping peacefully.

'You need to sleep too, darling,' he insisted, taking her hand and carefully lowering himself onto the bed so as not to jar her. 'You have to be exhausted.'

Amanda-Jayne shook her head. 'I'm too happy to sleep. Oh, Reb, he's perfect, isn't he?'

'How could he not be with you as his mother?' he said. 'I don't know what I did to deserve you in my life, A.J., but I'll be eternally glad God noted it.' With the back of his hand he stroked her cheek. 'You're the best thing to ever happen to me, A.J. I can't even bear to think what my life would be like without you. Promise me you'll never leave me...'

Fighting tears and the effects of the pain-killers she'd recently taken, Amanda-Jayne forced a smile. 'I love you so much my soul bleeds at the idea of being parted from you just until tomorrow morning, Reb Browne. My heart will have stopped before I could even think of leaving you.'

Leaning forward, Reb kissed her tenderly. A tear fell from his eyes onto her cheek as he drew back. How she managed to unerringly lift a finger to touch his tear amid her own he didn't know, but even more amazing was what she did next. Holding the tear on the finger of one hand, she carefully opened her nightie with the other; when the task was completed she gently touched the teardrop to her nipple.

'That's so both your strength and your tenderness will nurture your son in your absence,' she told him, taking his hand and holding it against her heart. 'I love you, Reb. If our son turns out to be half as kind, honourable and loving as you, I'll be the proudest mother alive.' She smiled. 'Heaven knows, I'm already the proudest wife.'

EPILOGUE

IF AMANDA-JAYNE was surprised to come home from hospital and find her beloved car sitting in the driveway with a bow around it, it was nothing compared to the surprise Reb had for her three years later on their shared thirtieth birthday.

'Reb Browne, there'd better be a very good reason why you're dragging me into the garage at one minute past midnight,' she grumbled, unable to think what he could possibly be keeping hidden here since there wasn't a new car, which had been her first guess. Her humouring mood started to further evaporate when he merely continued to grin silently.

'If this is an April Fool's joke…' she said ominously.

'It's not.' He opened the back door of the four-by-four and motioned her to get in.

'Are you nuts? Reb, I'm not going anywhere in my nightdress.'

'Don't worry, you won't be wearing it long,' he said, lifting her into the car then climbing in after her and shutting the door.

'Reb…what are you doing?'

His hand went to her neck. 'Re-creating my misspent youth.' His voice was lazy, his eyes full of mischief and desire. 'I racked my brains to think of a gift I could give you that wouldn't be overshadowed by the inheritance you're going to come into today. Then I remembered there was one thing you always said you wanted…'

He eased her onto her back and leaned over to blanket her body with his. 'By rights I should have made you climb

183

in here from the front seat, but a lady like you deserves better than that.'

The entire situation was so sweet, so crazy, so *typical* of how Reb continually surprised her that Amanda-Jayne was blinking back tears even as she laughed.

'Oh, darling! I love you! But we *can't* do this now.'

He produced a mock frown. 'Now that's a classic opening line if a guy has you in the back seat... Are you *sure* you haven't done this before?'

She tugged his ear hard. 'Yes! But I know *you* have!'

Grinning, he traced her clavicle and in the process slipped the straps of her nightdress off her shoulders. 'Jealous?'

'I refuse to answer on the grounds I may incriminate myself,' she said, then added more seriously, 'Reb, we won't hear Travis if he wakes, out here.'

'I told Savvy she was on toddler-sitting duty for the next three hours. So just relax and enjoy your birthday present, okay?'

Amanda-Jayne sighed as his mouth claimed hers and she was swept up in a kiss that left her boneless with love, desire and passion. It would have been infinitely easy to simply surrender to the magic of the moment right then, but there was something she wanted to do first so she forced herself to break the kiss.

'Er, I might as well give you your present now too. But I have to warn you, it's not as original as the one you're giving me and much more expensive. In fact,' she said, stifling a grin at his rueful expression, 'you're going to be paying for it for the next eighteen years at least.'

Amanda-Jayne counted three heartbeats before understanding dawned on Reb's handsome face.

'You're pregnant!' His delight was tangible as he grasped her to him. 'Oh, honey! That's great! It's— I'm...I'm—' Grinning widely, he shook his head. 'Oh, hell, I don't know what to say!'

She laughed. 'Well, good! That beats having you deny

responsibility the way you did when I told you about Travis! Now, if you're through looking so damned pleased with yourself, can we get back to *my* pres—?'

He cut her words off with a hard, possessive kiss that fed all of her senses and emotions to a point where she could scarcely think.

'Oh, God, A.J.... I love you, so much,' he rasped, against her throat. 'So damnably much. I can't tell you how much... I can't show you how much...'

'You don't have to, Reb,' she whispered. 'You've already given me the most precious things I ever have or ever will possess. You don't have to prove your love to me... Just *keep* loving me...'

'I will.'

'I know.'

MILLS & BOON®

Makes any time special

Enjoy a romantic novel from
Mills & Boon®

Presents... ™ *Enchanted* ™ *Temptation* ®

Historical Romance ™   *Medical Romance* ™

MILLS & BOON®

Next Month's Romance Titles

♡

Each month you can choose from a wide variety of romance novels from Mills & Boon®. Below are the new titles to look out for next month from the Presents...™ and Enchanted™ series.

Presents...™

A RELUCTANT MISTRESS	Robyn Donald
THE MARRIAGE RESOLUTION	Penny Jordan
THE FINAL SEDUCTION	Sharon Kendrick
THE REVENGE AFFAIR	Susan Napier
THE HIRED HUSBAND	Kate Walker
THE MILLIONAIRE AFFAIR	Sophie Weston
THE BABY VERDICT	Cathy Williams
THE IMPATIENT GROOM	Sara Wood

Enchanted™

THE DADDY DILEMMA	Kate Denton
AND MOTHER MAKES THREE	Liz Fielding
TO CLAIM A WIFE	Susan Fox
THE BABY WISH	Myrna Mackenzie
MARRYING A MILLIONAIRE	Laura Martin
THE HUSBAND CAMPAIGN	Barbara McMahon
TEMPTING A TYCOON	Leigh Michaels
MAIL-ORDER MARRIAGE	Margaret Way

On sale from 1st October 1999

H1 9909

Available at most branches of WH Smith, Tesco, Asda, Martins, Borders, Easons, Volume One/James Thin and most good paperback bookshops

Our hottest

TEMPTATION

authors bring you…

**Three sizzling love stories available in
one volume in September 1999.**

Midnight Heat
JoAnn Ross

A Lark in the Dark
Heather MacAllister

Night Fire
Elda Minger

MILLS & BOON®

Makes any time special™

By Request™

Bestselling themed romances brought back to you by popular demand

Each month By Request brings you three full-length novels in one beautiful volume featuring the best of the best.

So if you missed a favourite Romance the first time around, here is your chance to relive the magic from some of our most popular authors.

Look out for
Wedlocked **in September 1999 featuring Day Leclaire, Margaret Way and Anne McAllister**

CATHERINE LANIGAN
in love's
SHADOW

ON A COLD DECEMBER EVENING, A SHOT
RANG OUT IN A WEALTHY CHICAGO SUBURB
AND THE LIVES OF THREE WOMEN WERE
CHANGED FOREVER. BUD PULASKI, SUC-
CESSFUL BUSINESSMAN, COMMITTED SUI-
CIDE, LEAVING BEHIND A SHATTERED WIFE,
AN ESTRANGED SISTER, A BITTER MISTRESS
AND MANY UNANSWERED QUESTIONS.

THEY ARE THREE WOMEN—SEARCHING FOR
ANSWERS THAT WILL AFFECT THE REST OF
THEIR LIVES. SEARCHING FOR A RAY OF
HOPE IN LOVE'S SHADOW.

Published 17th September 1999

FREE
4 BOOKS
AND A SURPRISE GIFT!

We would like to take this opportunity to thank you for reading this Mills & Boon® book by offering you the chance to take FOUR more specially selected titles from the Presents...™ series absolutely FREE! We're also making this offer to introduce you to the benefits of the Reader Service™—

★ FREE home delivery   ★ FREE gifts and competitions
★ FREE monthly Newsletter   ★ Exclusive Reader Service discounts
★ Books available before they're in the shops

Accepting these FREE books and gift places you under no obligation to buy; you may cancel at any time, even after receiving your free shipment. Simply complete your details below and return the entire page to the address below. **You don't even need a stamp!**

YES! Please send me 4 free Presents... books and a surprise gift. I understand that unless you hear from me, I will receive 6 superb new titles every month for just £2.40 each, postage and packing free. I am under no obligation to purchase any books and may cancel my subscription at any time. The free books and gift will be mine to keep in any case.

P9EC

Ms/Mrs/Miss/Mr ....Initials ....
BLOCK CAPITALS PLEASE

Surname ....

Address ....

....

....Postcode ....

Send this whole page to:
UK: FREEPOST CN81, Croydon, CR9 3WZ
EIRE: PO Box 4546, Kilcock, County Kildare (stamp required)

Anne Mather

Wild Concerto

Fate forced Lani St John to make an impossible
choice, for Jake Pendragon, the man she had
loved from afar for years had re-entered her
life. Her desire for Jake was both a delight and
a torment because the beautiful rival—with
whom he was rumoured to be involved—was
none other than Lani's own mother!

Available from September 1999